It took a

CATASTROPHE

TO SET THEIR FATES IN MOTION . . .

Lillian Bryant . . . a beautiful nurse fighting to keep the man she loved, Dr. Dean Warner.

Dr. Dean Warner . . . he had too many secrets for his own health.

Carmen Ellsworth . . . elegant, vain, ambitious. What was her hold over Dr. Warner?

Howard Ellsworth . . . the disillusioned husband who finally found what he wanted: Lillian Bryant.

Vernon Jessup . . . he used the woman who loved him to win her roommate . . . Lillian Bryant.

Other Nurse-Doctor SIGNETS

HEARTBREAK NURSE

by Jane Converse

A SIGNET BOOK

Published by
THE NEW AMERICAN LIBRARY

Copyright © 1968 by Jane Converse

SIGNET TRADEMARK REG. U.S. PAT. OFF. AND FOREIGN COUNTRIES
REGISTERED TRADEMARK—MARCA REGISTRADA
HECHO EN CHICAGO, U.S.A.

SIGNET BOOKS are published by
The New American Library, Inc.,
1301 Avenue of the Americas, New York, New York 10019

FIRST PRINTING, DECEMBER, 1968

PRINTED IN THE UNITED STATES OF AMERICA

CHAPTER ONE

Around the wards at Tri-City Hospital, Lillian Bryant reflected, the R.N. with whom she shared this apartment was so mousy and nondescript that she almost blended into the ecru-painted walls. Yet here at home, especially when she was entertaining an eligible male, Bertha glittered like an ornate Christmas tree ornament.

Not that the thirtyish, birdlike little nurse managed to overcome her scrawny figure (which earned her the ludicrous nickname of "Big Bertha") or that her pinched face appeared any more glamorous with the off-duty addition of emerald eyeshadow and a thick coating of luminescent orchid-colored lipstick. Bertha's hair, in spite of investments in every gadget or preparation on the market which promised glistening waves, always reverted to its natural stringiness. Tonight it hung to her shoulders in steam-straightened wisps; Bertha had spent the time since her 7 A.M. to 3 P.M. shift cooking up a furious storm in the kitchen. Currently, her hair was dyed a curious shade that hovered between mulberry and maroon. Her matching "at home lounge ensemble," which had eaten up the best part of last week's salary, hung from Bertha's sparse figure dejectedly.

Seated at the dinette table between her friend and Tri-City's colorless administrator, Vernon Jessup, Lillian gave thought to analyzing the unique, almost chemical transformation that made "Big Bertha" come alive at times like this. It was her crying need, Lillian concluded. Facing a possible lifetime of living alone, Bertha poured a supercharge of energy into any contact that might end at the altar. Her green eyes shone brightly. Laughter and charm radiated from her. Bertha at the hospital was the plain, drab, efficient Miss Risdon, R.N.; here she was a determined woman with a purpose.

In Lillian's eyes, the object of this transformation was hardly inspiring. Vernon Jessup was known by the less charitable nurses at Tri-City as an "amiable clod." A more generous person would have noted that Vernon was a massive though reasonably presentable man with curly black hair, dark and solemn eyes, and a tendency toward middle-aged pudginess around the middle, though he was not yet out of his thirties. If you didn't require a sense of humor in a man, and had no objection to insipid conversation, Vernon was probably as good a marriage prospect as anyone around. And Bertha had long ago given up such stringent qualifications.

This evening, with his food-loving spirit buoyed by the epicurean dinner Bertha had worked on for four hours, Vernon was as animated and talkative as he was ever likely to be. "I'll never forget that afternoon," he was saying between bites of key lime pie. Somehow, they had gotten on the subject of Lillian's first job application. "There I was, sitting at my desk, wondering what else we could do to lure a few more good R.N.'s to Tri-City. We had our regular classified ads in the Phoenix newspapers. I'd sent out our regular job offers to every nursing school in the Southwest well before graduation. But, as always, we were still operating with a short staff."

"And that's when Lillian dropped in," Bertha grinned. "All out of a clear blue sky. Her diploma clutched in her hot little hand."

"Yes, and all my worldly goods checked into a

6

locker at the Phoenix bus station," Lillian remembered. "I hadn't even found a place to stay. Going on the theory that I couldn't risk paying rent anywhere until I'd found a job. Actually, you know, I was on my way to Los Angeles. I had no reason to stay in Chicago after I got my degree. There weren't any. . . ."

She came close to explaining why she had decided to leave the only area she had ever called home. Bertha already knew—and it was none of Vernon Jessup's business—that for the eighteen years since her parents had died in an automobile crash, home, for Lillian, had been a series of short stays with indifferent foster parents. Her three-year struggle to get through nursing school, while supplementing a small scholarship by working in a hospital cafeteria, was another series of dreary episodes that wouldn't liven after-dinner conversation. She had been too busy or too exhausted during most of that time for dates, and her only friends, budding nurses like herself, would scatter after graduation. Lillian had decided upon Arizona or California because of their mild climates, not because she knew a soul in either state. Hard to believe that a year had gone by. Late in June again. And no closer to realizing the romantic dreams that had propelled her westward. No closer. Although now she could no longer say that she was a stranger to love. . . .

Lillian shook herself out of the melancholy reverie, suddenly conscious that she had stopped talking in midsentence and that the others were politely waiting for her to finish. Lillian released an embarrased laugh. "I don't even know the name of the old woman who suggested that I stop off in Phoenix. She lives out here in the suburbs somewhere. Anyway, she told me about this new hospital and. . . ." Lillian shrugged. "I was getting bus-weary, so I decided to get off and try my luck."

Vernon raised his coffee cup in what was, for him, an uncommonly frivolous gesture. "A toast to that unnamed lady on the bus. For steering a badly needed and very naive R.N. to my office." The broad face widened for an instant in a smile, also uncommon. "I couldn't believe that you were actually afraid you'd be turned down. And there I was, trying to sell you the advantages of living in the sun. I believe . . . yes, I actually *did* check the bulletin board next to the nurses' lounge. Told you about Bertha wanting someone to share her apartment. I remember making a point to mention the swimming pool . . . I hoped that would impress you. Then, even after we'd talked about your state board exam, you still weren't sure you were hired. You'd heard there was a nursing shortage, surely?"

"It seemed too good to be true, I guess. A real job. Doing the kind of work I'd always wanted to do, having money of my own to spend." Lillian hesitated once more. No point in recalling the years of hand-me-down clothes, rooms which were hers only by the grace of charity, meals that had to be skipped because textbooks and uniforms had priority. She looked across the table, out to the lighted courtyard of the sprawling U-shaped adobe building. The glass-walled dining area was framed by bougainvillea vines, brilliant with masses of magenta blossoms. Beyond the window, flanked by towering fan palms, a flagstoned terrace invited you out to relax on floral-printed lounges. At night, the lighted pool which centered the court sparkled like a turquoise gem. "I'm still impressed," Lillian said. She turned her gaze away from the scene outside to smile at Bertha. "If I hadn't been sold when you took me on a tour of the hospital, Vernon, I'd have been convinced when I saw this place. More than that —when I met Bertie, here, that afternoon."

Bertha pretended annoyance. "Well, if anybody can get into this mutual admiration society, let me tell you it was a break for me, too. I can't afford this apartment alone. After all, this *is* a pretty posh resort area.

So let me tell you about the last three gals who shared the place with me." Bertha paused to offer Vernon more pie. Her questioning expression was answered by a shake of his head and a contented tummy pat—the silent communication of two people who might have, to all appearances, been married to each other for a decade. "One was an emergency room nurse who worked on the night shift and got home in time to give me all the gruesome details with my breakfast. Lucy Sherrill . . . you remember her, Vernon."

"Got married and left us," was what Vernon remembered in a grudging tone.

"Yeah. Well, after ole blood-an'-gore left, I went through two more in a hurry. The gal from Personnel was a corker. Taking electric guitar lessons was okay, but did she have to be so diligent? Twang, twang, twang . . . and if *she* wasn't practicing, her boyfriend was over here cleaning out the refrigerator and playing those awful records until all hours." Bertha raised her eyes to stare prayerfully at the ceiling for a moment. *"That* one I invited to leave. The gal just before Lillian didn't have to be asked to leave. She was a . . . I guess she told me she worked as a hostess, but that's probably a polite term for hanging around bars and seeing what comes up. Point is, I came home one day to find her gone. Along with a few sundry items, like my hair dryer and my luggage. She owed me two months' rent, incidentally."

Vernon made a sympathetic sound with his tongue.

"After that, I made up my mind I'd accept Tri-City nurses *only*. Preferably one who didn't work in Emergency and feel obligated to give me a stitch-by-stitch account of every accident case." Bertha beamed approval at her most recent selection. "Lillian doesn't take her job home with her."

"She doesn't have to," Vernon said. Lillian braced herself for a flood of the unctuous flattery that was the administrator's trademark. "She does the best possible job at the hospital, where it's important. And she's sensible enough to get away from her work afterwards —enjoy her free hours and come back to her patients refreshed."

Bertha's face wrinkled in a dubious scowl. "I can't agree with the bit about enjoying her free hours, but I'll buy the business about going back to work feeling rested. When you don't do anything but mope around this apartment, it's probably a relief to go to work in the morning. At least you aren't bored at the hospital."

Vernon emitted a short laugh, indicating that the opposite was probably true. "I'm sure Lillian doesn't find time to get bored. On the contrary, I would have expected complaints from her head nurse. Pretty girls have a way of staying up late, going out on too many dates . . ."

Lillian darted an annoyed glance at her friend for bringing up the uncomfortable subject. It was annoying enough to have Bertha badgering her because she never went out—because she was so hopelessly in love with a doctor who barely knew she existed that other men held no appeal for her at all. Bertha's familiar lectures on the subject ("You're wasting your life mooning about Dean Warner"—"So you're in love with that cold fish. Does that mean you have to vegetate?") were troublesome enough. But even worse was this assumption on Vernon's part that her life was one delirious round of dates, parties, and panting admirers. It would not be so, even if she had not taken what Bertha called a "perverse vow of lonely spinsterdom"; during the past year, there had been a show of interest by the few unmarried doctors, technicians, and even patients at Tri-City. Lately, since her aloofness was probably assumed, the invitations had all but ceased. Since she had not expanded her social horizons beyond the hospital, Lillian no longer *expected* the invitations. Her reasons were painful and sensitive; the last person she wanted exploring her life was this drab, proper, unimaginative man at her side.

Perhaps Vernon Jessup had guessed more than she wanted him to know. Or perhaps Bertha had unwittingly verified a suspicion that buzzed along the hospital grapevine. Or was it only a logical coincidence that he was mentioning Dr. Warner now? "In Administration, we can always evaluate a nurse by the number of special requests our attending physicians make for her services. I know that Dr. Warner has had you taken off general duty every time he has a patient who needs meticulous care. Upsets Mrs. Hayden's schedule, but she's given up reminding him that we have Private Duty nurses available for that purpose." Vernon popped an after-dinner mint into his mouth. "You should feel flattered, Lillian. We all know what a stickler for perfection Warner is. Regular walking medical machine. Which just may explain his extremely successful practice. And there's no question that he's partial to you when he's very concerned about a patient."

It was true. In fact, there had been a brief period when Lillian had been more than flattered by the doctor's preference for her services: She had been encouraged to hope that his interest in her went beyond his respect for her efficiency, her dedication as a nurse. The hope had been short-lived. Apart from routine doctor-to-nurse instructions, he had never spoken to her; even his appreciation, after a patient was recovered and released, was taken for granted.

Bertha was beginning to share Lillian's discomfort. This was *her* evening, after all. She had, in her own words, "knocked herself out" preparing a gourmet dinner. She looked forward to being alone with this highly eligible, if unglamorous, marriage prospect. It seemed unfair to ask her to listen to Vernon's glowing praise of another woman. Lillian checked her watch, remembering that she had assured her friend that she would leave the apartment immediately after dinner. This was

11

to be an at-home date for Bertha, during which she would undoubtedly try to impress Vernon with the advantages of relaxing in a cozy, female-brightened living room. It was too early to head for Lillian's only refuge, the local movie house, and, besides, an abrupt departure would have seemed too obvious. She would have to endure the conversation for at least twenty minutes more; it was only humane to turn the spotlight away from herself.

As casually as possible, Lillian said, "All the doctors seem to have their favorites, don't they? I know Dr. Buell would rather have Bertha on a case than me."

"Yes. Well, Buell's in his seventies," Vernon said. With all the delicacy of a runaway bulldozer, he added his tactless explanation: "Old men like that associate young, pretty girls with frivolity. He'd naturally prefer a . . . more mature type. More . . ." He apparently realized that saying "plain" would have been resented. Vernon settled for mumbling, "More responsible looking."

Lillian was rescued from Bertha's hurt expression and the administrator's bumbling embarrassment by the ringing telephone. She leaped up from her chair. "I'll get it."

Several minutes later, she dropped the receiver into its cradle and turned to the others. They could not have helped overhearing her end of the conversation.

"You're wanted at the hospital *now?*" Bertha frowned. "You've already put in eight hours . . ."

"It's . . . an emergency," Lillian said. (She felt shaky, suddenly, and puzzled by the urgency in the head nurse's voice: "*Doctor wants you here as fast as possible.*") "Dr. Warner's patient. An accident of some kind."

"We have a perfectly capable emergency-room staff," Vernon protested. "I'm going to take up this business of overtime requests with the Board at our next. . . ."

"I don't mind," Lillian told him. She excused herself and raced to her room.

In a few minutes she would be at Dean Warner's side, helping him, being close to him, giving him the only part of herself that he seemed willing to accept: her skill and devotion as a nurse. Always, when he summoned her, Lillian dropped whatever she was doing and ran. This time, for no reason except some vague, undefined, intuitive stirring inside herself, she could not hurry fast enough.

CHAPTER TWO

Amy Casady, who served as Tri-City's head nurse on the surgical floor during the second shift, was one of those people who defy description simply because there are no distinguishing characteristics to describe. Neither young nor old, fat nor thin, stern nor sunny, Mrs. Casady's conservative hairdo and makeup, her quiet, uniformly polite manner, and her indeterminate age (Lillian's guess was somewhere between thirty and fifty) helped to blend the woman into the impersonal atmosphere of the charge desk.

Either because she was not given to showing her emotions or because she was superbly trained, Mrs. Casady could report a major catastrophe or request cream for her coffee with the same calm and unhesitating voice. It was for this reason that her breathless manner when Lillian reported for duty, confirmed Lillian's earlier intuition: This was no ordinary case. Yet Mrs. Casady seemed unable to supply more than the most meager details. "I can only tell you, Miss Bryant, that the patient is a little five-year-old girl." The head nurse checked her admission form on the desk. "Her name is Patty Ellsworth. She was brought in more dead than alive, mangled by a . . . machine of some kind."

"An automobile?"

Mrs. Casady shook her head, and Lillian detected a shuddering motion. "No, a . . . tractor or . . . some

14

piece of construction equipment. I'm not sure. I do know her condition is critical."

"How awful!" Lillian gave an unconscious glance toward the third-floor reception room. "Are her parents in the room now?"

"She's still in Surgery," Mrs. Casady said, as though that explained why the child's parents weren't visible. "Dr. Warner will explain what he wants of you when he comes out of the O.R., I expect. He's there with Dr. Corbett and Dr. Laing and Dr. Severson and Dr. Stein and. . . ." The head nurse had rattled off the name of every prominent surgeon and internist in the area before she stopped, adding unnecessarily, "Dr. Warner's extremely concerned about this patient. I've never seen him so upset."

Nothing was making sense. "Upset" was not a word that applied to the general practitioner Lillian had learned to love at a distance. Dr. Warner was *always* concerned, *always* thorough, and no one ever questioned that a patient entrusted to him was given the most conscientious care available within the profession. But though compassion often glazed his deep blue eyes, no colleague—and certainly no patient—had ever seen him visibly "upset." Lillian expressed her surprise. "That's not like him, is it, Mrs. Casady?"

"It's not like him to shout at the nursing staff in Emergency, either," the other woman confided. "Or to snap at a respected specialist like Dr. Corbett. Especially since he called him in personally."

Evidently Mrs. Casady decided that she had already broken too many rules of ethics, because she ended her recital soon afterward to tell Lillian that Dr. Warner had made a personal request for *her* presence, too. Not in Emergency or Surgery, but, optimistically, to serve as a Special during the critical night shift. "He's determined the child is going to survive," Mrs. Casady concluded. "I imagine he wanted you here this early so that he can acquaint you with the case."

15

"He called me in *four hours* before I'm to go on duty?"

"I told you he's upset. *Personally* upset would be my guess." Mrs. Casady released a disconsolate sigh. "It's only that, of course: my guess. But I've only seen doctors behave the way he's behaving when the patient is . . . close to them. Not that Dr. Warner wouldn't do everything possible to save the life of a perfect stranger. Especially a small child. He's terribly disturbed, though. It's only fair to warn you, Miss Bryant, that if you take the case . . . apart from the difficulties . . . the seriousness of the injuries . . . you'll have to exercise the greatest patience with. . . ."

Mrs. Casady's sentence was left hanging, as the swinging doors of the O.R. down the hall were opened. A gurney was wheeled out by two nurses and an orderly. A doctor Lillian recognized as the hospital's Chief Anesthetist followed. She caught her breath at the sight of Dr. Warner. Walking beside the small still form on the rolling stretcher, still wearing a green surgical gown and cap, he reflected none of the strong confidence that was so typical of him. Even at a distance, he appeared more like a layman stunned by fear than the doctor in charge.

As the little patient was wheeled past the nurses' station on her way to Recovery, Mrs. Casady stepped out from behind the charge desk. Lillian didn't hear the quiet words the head nurse addressed to Dr. Warner.

Barely hesitating, as though he were reluctant to let the child out of his sight even for an instant, Dr. Warner said, "We didn't have to amputate the left arm, thank God. We may need more blood." His voice quavered. "Tell her parents she came through Surgery." A few yards down the corridor, he turned back without breaking step. "Did you contact Miss Bryant?" He had not noticed Lillian as he passed the charge desk.

"She's here now, Doctor." Mrs. Casady followed the gurney for a few steps. "Dr. Warner? I haven't seen the patient's parents. Do you know where . . ."

"How in hell am I supposed to know where they are?" he shrilled.

Mrs. Casady gasped audibly. The nurses and the Anesthetist exchanged apprehensive glances. The little girl was still unconscious; she could not have heard him. But the doctor's strident cry echoed through the long hallway. *"Maybe they ran out for a drink. Out making some more money. I don't know. That's what you're getting paid to do. Find them!"*

Mrs. Casady's mumbled, "Yes, doctor" was more sorrowful than resentful. She walked past Lillian, returning to her desk to pick up the telephone. "I can't imagine where. . . ." She interrupted herself to tell Lillian, "I doubt the doctor will be talking to you for awhile. He'll want to stay with the patient until. . . ." The head nurse cut off this sentence, too. "It doesn't look too promising, I'm afraid. Why don't you go downstairs for some coffee? When Dr. Warner wants you, I'll call you there."

"I've just finished with dinner, thanks. If you don't mind, I'll wait here."

Mrs. Casady was talking into the telephone, asking a receptionist if a Mr. and Mrs. Ellsworth were in the main-floor waiting room, when Lillian changed her mind. The staff dining hall would be almost deserted by now, but there was always the chance of meeting someone she knew in the public coffee shop near the hospital entrance. Conversation would pass the time and ease her unaccountable nervousness. Signalling to Mrs. Casady, who acknowledged her understanding by a nod of her head, Lillian started for the elevator. Two of the doctors who had participated in the emergency operation on Patty Ellsworth rode down to the first floor with her.

17

"Didn't Dean want you to stay?" one of them asked the other.

The latter, Dr. Buell, pursed his lips to make a perplexed hooshing sound. "There's absolutely nothing more I can do, Fred. Except try to talk Dean into taking a sedative. He's on the verge of collapse. Almost hysterical. Frankly, I found it unnerving to have him in the O.R."

The other doctor threw him a warning glance, reminding him that they were in the presence of a nurse. "That poor little thing! Pleural cavity crushed . . . it's a miracle her heart and lungs weren't damaged."

For a few seconds, they talked in medical terms that Lillian guessed were deliberately phrased to escape her understanding. She gathered that the child had nearly lost an arm, that four ribs had been smashed, and that the loss of blood had added extreme shock to the list of traumata. It was evident that neither of the doctors was overly optimistic. As they hurried out of the elevator cage on the first-floor level, Dr. Buell was saying, "I've learned not to underestimate faith. Everything points to a discouraging prognosis except Dean's determination. He *can't* let that child die. He won't accept. . . ."

They were out of earshot as Lillian turned into the glass-walled coffee shop. As usual, during the evening visiting hours, the cheerful yellow floral plastic stools that lined the counter were occupied. Only two visitors were allowed into the hospital rooms at a time; relatives alternated, using the coffee shop as a meeting-place.

Lillian looked around for a familiar face among the people seated in the booths, recognized no one, and took her place near the counter; the teen-aged girl who was finishing her Coke would probably be leaving soon, she guessed.

Waiting, still hopeful of finding someone to talk with, Lillian found herself, once again, an unintentional eavesdropper. Reluctant to turn around, she heard a deep, expansive male voice arguing, "So I've told you I'm sorry. You think I'm happy about it? You think it was a pleasure, untangling the kid from that scraper . . . rushing down here with my foreman holding her in his lap, yelling at me she was bleeding to death? I had the accelerator down to the floorboard. I had that Caddie going a hundred and . . ."

"Will you stop trying to be a hero?" The female voice that had cut in was husky, the words carefully enunciated, and yet there was a sharp, cutting edge to the woman's tone. "If you had been watching Pat . . ."

"I just turned around for a second! Look, I'm busy on the project. I can't supervise two million dollars worth of construction and baby-sit at the same time. If you hadn't fired the maid, if you were home where you're supposed to be . . ."

"You know I had an important audition!" The woman's voice rose above the coffee-shop chatter and the soft buzz of other conversations and was now high-pitched and accusing. "Letting her play around those horrible machines! My baby. . . ."

"Your baby!" The words were repeated in a scathing monotone. "Why aren't you upstairs right now if you're so concerned about your baby? You heard what Dean said."

"He said he's going to save her." There was a pause, followed by a thin, sniffling sound. After a few seconds, the woman whimpered, "Don't be cruel, Howard. Haven't you done enough? You know how sensitive I am. If I saw Pat . . . if I had to see her before they . . . oh, dammit, you know I can't stand anything gruesome! Her arm. Dean said her arm was almost torn off. My beautiful little doll!"

"Don't you think we ought to at least call upstairs and see if your beautiful little doll is out of the operating room?" The male voice, thick with disgust, softened as he muttered, "This isn't pleasant for me, either, you know. I feel guilty as hell. We *both* ought to feel guilty as hell."

Lillian waited until the man had stepped up to the cashier's booth. Pretending that she had not overheard their conversation, she moved toward the cash register.

The man was huge, as big and broad as his rumbling bass voice. He was dressed in an obviously expensive lightweight suit. His rough-hewn, tanned features were capped by a thick crop of curly, rust-colored hair. For a few seconds, as Lillian approached, his dark eyes inspected her with cool hostility.

"Excuse me," she said. "Would you happen to be Mr. Ellsworth?"

He grunted an affirmative reply. Probably drawn by curiosity, his wife edged back from the glass exit door to join him. Apart from the pages of fashion magazines, Lillian had never seen a more stunning woman. Tall, chic, professionally poised, the brunette hardly filled Lillian's image of an anguished mother.

"The head nurse on the surgical floor is trying to reach you," she told the couple.

Mrs. Ellsworth's lacquered fingers shot to her face. "Patty isn't . . . she's not . . . ?"

"No. I'm not authorized to give you a medical report," Lillian said. "I do know that your little girl came through surgery and she's in the recovery room now. Dr. Warner is with her."

Mr. Ellsworth had not quite lost his suspicious attitude. He struck Lillian as a man who assumed that everyone on earth was out to do him in and that he didn't dare let down his guard for a moment. His expression wary, he asked if it would be possible to see the little girl.

Before Lillian could explain that the child would probably be in Recovery for some time and that patients could not be visited during this crucial period, Mrs. Ellsworth cut in. "I couldn't bear to see her yet.

When they get her to her room . . . where she's all . . . covered and. . . ." She looked up at her husband helplessly. "You know what I mean, Howard."

"My wife can't stand anything . . . you know. . . ." Mr. Ellsworth's face, although deeply tanned, colored visibly. "You nurses are used to seeing all kinds of . . . you know what I mean. I know I nearly fainted myself, bringing the kid here. I guess we'd rather . . . well, it's better if we wait for awhile." Eager to justify what may have been interpreted as callousness or indifference, he added hastily, "We'll be right nearby. We want to know what's happening. We're very worried."

"I'm sure you are," Lillian said. She tried to attribute Mrs. Ellsworth's attitude to shock yet she could not escape feeling a twinge of disgust. Usually, mothers had to be *restrained* from being with their children; every normal instinct drove them to the injured child's side, even when their presence might interfere with medical procedures. Lillian had found herself in the restraining position more than once during the past year; it was one of the problems a nursing staff coped with sympathetically, but firmly, for the patient's sake. Yet, as much as hysterical relatives upset the efficiency of a hospital, they were understandable and human. They deserved more respect than this icily perfect woman who had not let tears mar her perfectly applied mascara and whose selfish concern for her own sensibilities exceeded her desire to be with her child.

Lillian did her best to copy Mrs. Casady's impassive manner as the willowy brunette said, "It's been a terrible shock. I could use a drink. Suppose . . . do you think we could wait at the Clarion Hotel cocktail lounge?" Her aqua-gray eyes implored Lillian's understanding. "You could call us there, in case we're needed, couldn't you? The atmosphere here is so depressing, and, really, I'm . . . I'm terribly nervous. It's been so . . . dreadful!"

Lillian assured the woman she would deliver that message to the charge desk. She was politely thanked by Mr. Ellsworth, and she waited in the coffee shop until she had seen the elegantly dressed couple go out through the hospital's revolving glass doors.

The red-haired cashier, who had evidently been listening attentively, looked after the Ellsworths with a smirking expression. "Takes all kinds," she said to Lillian. Then, noticing that one of the customers was getting ready to leave the counter, she said, "There's a place for you, hon."

Lillian shook her head. "I don't think I want anything," she said. She left the cashier staring after her as she made her way back toward the elevators.

CHAPTER THREE

Room 406, to which Patty Ellsworth was wheeled shortly before eleven o'clock that night, seemed to have become the focal point of Tri-City Hospital. Although Lillian, as the child's Special Duty Nurse, was ostensibly in charge, she spent no more than a few minutes alone with the tiny patient during the night-long shift. Doctors and nurses came and went, each making his or her contribution under the questioning surveillance of Dean Warner. Except for consultations with other physicians, the latter never left Patty's bedside. Lillian found her hands trembling under his watchful eyes. Hypertense, driving himself to exhaustion, he was like a man possessed.

During a lull in the visits from specialists the doctor had called in, Lillian made the gentle suggestion that Dr. Warner try to get some rest. She was unprepared for his hissing anger. "If you think you're qualified to take this case over, Miss Bryant, we might make other arrangements! You tell *me* what to do and I'll follow *your* orders!"

Lillian fought against the tears that rose in her eyes. "I don't want to give orders, Doctor. I just thought . . . the patient's resting quietly now. I promise not to take my eyes off her. If you're worn out tomorrow, you won't be able to . . ."

"I know my own endurance, thank you," he whispered sharply. His usually handsome face was contorted into an agonized mask; in the dim light he looked like a tormented old man.

For a long, breathless period, having exhausted every possible order that he could think of, Dr. Warner stood beside the bed without saying a word. Lillian checked the I.V. needle through which life saving blood trickled into the child's veins. She had been taking Patty Ellsworth's pulse and temperature at closely spaced intervals—yet never often enough to please the doctor. Now, satisfied that there was nothing she could do without disturbing the little girl's needed rest, she turned her gaze to Patty's waxen face.

Even for a child of five, the patient was rather small. Her face had miraculously escaped injury, considering that most of the rest of the fragile little body had been cut and bruised. Short, blond curls covered Patty's head; her hair was damp and dishevelled. In spite of this, she looked angelic in her sleep. Lillian wondered briefly about the color of her eyes and quickly rejected a negative thought: In a seriously injured patient this pallor and peacefulness often presaged death.

Was Dr. Warner thinking the same thing? Lillian lifted her stare to see that the doctor's eyes were moist. His lips moved, as if in silent prayer. It was an unorthodox thing for a nurse to say to the physician in charge, but Lillian found the words escaping her: "She's going to be all right. I just know she is!"

A nurse didn't offer such flimsily based encouragement to despairing relatives; the alternatives were too cruel to permit the raising of false hopes. And this was not a desperate parent; this was an M.D. who, more than anyone else, knew the gravity of the situation. For a frightening instant, Lillian expected the doctor to lash out at her again, to remind her that nurses didn't make statements founded on nothing more than wishful thinking.

Strangely, Dean Warner only nodded solemnly. He

gazed at the pale little face before him for another moment, and then, abruptly, he turned away and walked to the opposite side of the room. With his back turned toward her, Lillian caught the trembling of his shoulders. She would have sworn that the man was crying.

A few minutes afterward, composed, he was back at the bedside, his hushed voice brusquely efficient as he requested a pulse reading. He bit his lower lip as Lillian repeated the discouraging report; Patty Ellsworth's pulse remained feeble. Her lips had not lost their bluish tinge. Although most of her body was swathed in bandages, her doll-like hands lay exposed on top of the light covers; her fingers were cold to the touch.

Dr. Warner placed his stethoscope against the little girl's chest—his movements cautious and tender, aware of the child's shattered and taped ribs. He was on the phone an instant later, ordering medications, snapping at the charge nurse, who evidently questioned whether a Dr. Chalmers could be reached at that hour of the night. "Don't argue with me, Nurse! Get him over here!"

There followed a terrifying crisis during which Lillian was relegated to the role of a helpless onlooker, while Dr. Warner and two colleagues worked over the child. *Oxygen! Heart stimulants! Whole blood!* Floor nurses ran in and out of the room, jumping in response to Dr. Warner's hoarse commands. And once, during this crisis—which was to be followed by two others before the night was over—the consulting doctors learned that it was dangerous to even suggest that they might be fighting a losing battle. One of them triggered an angry scene with his pessimism.

Dr. Chalmers was an elderly man, recently retired from his position as Tri-City's Chief of Staff. As Patty's respiration seemed to halt, he expressed a solemn, regretful suggestion: "Don't you think your patient's parents ought to be here, Dr. Warner?" His long years of experience told him what to expect; he hinted at imminent death with sorrow in his voice.

"She isn't going to die!" Dr. Warner croaked. His words were barely audible—but his tone was vicious. "I don't want to hear anyone telling me Patty isn't going to pull through. Not even you, Dr. Chalmers! If you can't help me . . . if you're ready to give up . . ." his voice broke, but he didn't interrupt his desperate efforts. ". . . please get out of the room."

He mumbled a vague apology when the crisis was over. When the other doctors had left, he meekly acknowledged to Lillian that he might have been a little harsh with the old man. "Dr. Chalmers was only seeing Patty as a physician," he said senselessly.

Lillian didn't question him. "There are times," she assured Dr. Warner softly, "when medical knowledge isn't enough, is it? I felt so useless there for a while. Wanting to do so much, and . . . not able to do anything but pray."

The harsh lines of tension relaxed, and for a few seconds Dean Warner's eyes met Lillian's, still troubled, but touchingly gentle. "Is that what you were doing?" he asked.

Lillian nodded. Because he wanted so passionately to keep the spark of life alive in this tiny patient, and because he must have known how formidably the odds were stacked against him, he needed much more than her devotion as a nurse. She had never loved him as deeply. Even when his nerves had snapped, earlier, and his criticism had become abusive, she had only yearned for the right to put her arms around him, to comfort him, to assure him that she knew that he was doing all that any doctor could do—and more. Now the urge to reach out and touch his face was almost overpowering.

"*You* believe Patty's going to live, *don't* you?" Dr. Warner's question was a plea from the heart. "You won't let yourself doubt it for a second, *will* you?"

It was not the kind of question any doctor would ask a nurse. But the man she loved had said the words with an intensity that was almost palpable in the still room; it was an anguished demand for faith that could be felt, like some living thing that could not be denied.

"I believe," Lillian formed the words with her lips, surprised by the soundlessness of her promise.

For another instant, the pain-filled blue eyes remained locked with her own. Then, turning away and bending down to let his fingertips hover over Patty Ellsworth's face—as though he longed to touch her cheek but was afraid to disturb her mercifully drugged sleep —Dean Warner said, "Thank you, Miss Bryant. I knew I could depend on you."

At least he knows *that,* Lillian thought wearily when the night's ordeal was over. Dr. Warner was still in the room when the seven-to-three Special came to relieve her. He seemed reluctant to let Lillian go, and only her admission that she was exhausted brought forth his grudging, "Get plenty of sleep. We're not out of the woods yet." He waved aside her suggestion that he should rest, too.

At least he knows that he can count on me. The thought ran through Lillian's numbed senses as she drove home through the bright Arizona sunshine. Reviving her senses by taking deep breaths of the crisp desert air, she took what comfort there was to be found in knowing that, though she was not yet loved, she was now undeniably needed. Patty Ellsworth (there was no doubting it now) was more than an angelically beautiful child, more than a critically injured patient. In Dean Warner's eyes and heart, she was far more than that. It didn't matter why. All that mattered was a promise that she had given. "I believe," Lillian repeated aloud as she piloted her small car through the morning freeway traffic. Death, and the memory of a pathetically pale little face mocked her words. She had finished her night's duty as a nurse, but she was still urgently needed.

Fiercely, almost defiantly, she said the words again, drawing strength from them, and somehow sensing that their power would reach the quiet room where a tormented man kept his watch over a helpless child: *"I believe!"*

CHAPTER FOUR

If Bertha Risdon could offer no concrete solutions to the mystery of Dr. Warner's more-than-professional interest in his five-year-old patient, she was certainly able to provide details about the child's parents.

She had already left for the hospital when Lillian returned to their apartment, but shortly after three o'clock that afternoon, while the two of them sipped coffee by an umbrella-shaded tree in the patio, Bertha supplied every detail with which the hospital grapevine had buzzed throughout the morning shift.

"I talked to Peggy Loomis in the parking lot after I got off," Bertha began. "She's on your case—morning shift, right? She was pretty well beat, but she said that poor little kid is holding her own. That's all she said —'holding her own'. In a tone of voice that says the worst can happen and probably will. She thinks. . . ."

"I don't care *what* she thinks!" Lillian broke in angrily. "Patty's going to recover!"

Bertha eyed her warily. "Well, don't yell at *me!* I'm only telling you what the Special said."

"I'm sorry." Lillian sighed heavily. "I already knew Patty'd gotten through this far. I got up around two o'clock and I've called the desk several times since."

Bertha considered this admission of personal interest for a moment and then said, "I guess everybody's pulling for the little Ellsworth girl. It's such a . . . terrible thing. Everybody on the floor was talking about the case. It's so sad. I mean, even if she pulls through, she'll probably be badly crippled. . . ."

"She's going to be perfectly well!" This time, Lillian was astounded by the fury in her voice. She stirred her coffee savagely. "I get so irritated with all those negative gloom-peddlers, I. . . ."

"Hey, maybe you should have slept a few more hours," Bertha suggested. *"I* know it's a rough case. All the more reason you ought to stay in the sack a while longer. Recharge your batteries for tonight. I hear Warner isn't fit to be around. He's ready to drop, but he won't quit. Surviving on black coffee, Peggy told me. Boy! The two of you start snarling at each other tonight, you'll get thrown out of the hospital."

"Dr. Warner *can't* quit," Lillian said absently.

Bertha broke an English muffin in two. "So they tell me. You know what everybody thinks? He's carrying a great big torch for Carmen Ellsworth."

"Patty's mother?" Lillian scowled. "That's ridiculous."

"Have you ever *seen* the kid's mother?" Bertha asked.

"Sure, I've seen her. She's an exceptionally beautiful woman. Not my idea of a solicitous mother, but I won't deny that she's gorgeous. But she also happens to be married, and I think it's pretty cheap gossip if anyone's implying. . . ."

"You *are* in a huffy mood!" Bertha said. "All right. I was going to tell you what's going the rounds, but if you want to get defensive because somebody—who just might happen to know the score, incidentally—somebody suggested that Dean Warner is not the pure white knight you've made out of him in your daydreams, *well* . . . forget I said anything! Let me tell you about my wild, romantic evening with Vernon Jessup. Two glamorous games of checkers, two hours of thrilling Westerns on T.V., two intoxicating cups of cocoa. . . ."

"I don't want to hear about Vernon Jessup!" Lillian snapped. She stopped to take a deep breath, aware that the annoyance stirring her insides was inseparable from jealousy. When she was sure that she could sound self-possessed again, she said, "Is this just guesswork or does the rumor have some basis in fact?"

Bertha accepted that as an apology. "Evidently Dr. Warner has known Mrs. Ellsworth for a long time. That much is for sure. Nobody came right out and said they're . . . you know . . . anything more than friends. But, face it, Warner's too attractive a man not to have *any* women in his life. And he's the discreet type. If he *were* having an affair with a married woman—especially a woman who's in the public eye and has a reputation to guard—well, look—he'd keep it pretty quiet, wouldn't he?"

"Exactly what I thought," Lillian said adamantly. "Guesswork. Petty gossip. Pure imagination—and not very imaginative at that." She realized that her unencouraged love for the doctor was making her sound like an oversensitive, perhaps even bitter, old maid. "Okay. Maybe he *is* in love with Mrs. Ellsworth." She avoided a catty observation that had sprung into her mind: Dean Warner seemed more agonized about Patty's condition than the woman he wanted to save from grief. It was a difference in character, she decided. There was nothing in the book that said a warm, compassionate man could not fall in love with a vain selfish woman—especially if that woman drew stares as she walked into a room. "I've never heard of Carmen Ellsworth," Lillian said. "Is she a . . . show business personality? An actress, or. . . ."

"No, she runs a chain of modeling agencies and charm schools all over the Southwest," Bertha explained. "You've seen her on her own T.V. commercials, haven't you? And then she does an early afternoon show locally. Glamour tips . . . how to put on makeup and do your hair." It wasn't much of a recommendation, but Bertha added, "I used to watch her all the time when I worked the three-to-eleven shift. She really knows her business. Fact is, she used to be a professional model herself in New York. Then I guess she came back to Phoenix and married this wealthy building contractor. She had all kinds of money to spend, but one of the lab girls told me she got bored and started a modeling studio, and the business just took off and grew like crazy. So now she gives it about ninety percent of her time, and they say her husband's fit to be tied. Somebody said there's been talk of divorce—entirely apart from that other deal about Dr. Warner. . . ."

" '*They* say'," Lillian repeated derisively. " '*They* say'. '*Somebody* said'. Isn't that vicious? Two people have a tragic accident in the family. Their doctor— probably a good friend of *Mr.* Ellsworth's, too—*kills* himself to save their little girl. And what does the staff at Tri-City do? Invent the most malicious story imaginable. I think anyone who repeats one word of what you've been telling me ought to be thoroughly ashamed." Lillian set her coffee cup down with a clatter. "Maybe we'd better talk about your big evening with Vernon. You stayed here the whole time? Was that your idea or his?"

"You don't want to hear about it," Bertha said glumly. "For the record, nothing interesting happened. Except that he accepted another invitation to dinner next week." Bertha rose to gather up the china and teaspoons. "Big deal."

"He didn't offer to take you out? Not even to a movie?"

"Not even to a dogfight," Bertha admitted. She was carrying the dishes back into the kitchen, Lillian following her with the muffin tray, when Bertha found the single encouraging note in her doleful attempt at romance. "At least I don't have *your* problem. Vernon's so dull, I don't have to worry about competition from

32

some glamorpuss like Carmen Ellsworth. Who but a drip like me would *want* him?"

It was an obvious bid for reassurance, but Lillian was not in the mood to supply a pep talk. Before following Bertha into the kitchen, she would phone the third-floor desk at Tri-City once more.

What if the rumors were actually true? Dean Warner's reason for being more than professionally concerned about Patty Ellsworth might, in the long run, shatter a cherished dream. If he lost Patty, he would be tortured, as any doctor is tortured, when he loses the struggle to save a critically injured patient. But would he give and find solace in taking this child's mother into his arms? *It doesn't make any difference,* Lillian reminded herself. Seeing him win the battle was all that counted. Seeing that lovely child alive and well, bidding a smiling goodbye to Room 406—*that* was important. Carmen Ellsworth was a forgotten issue as Lillian dialed the familiar hospital number. When she dropped the receiver less than a minute later, she breathed a silent prayer of thanks.

CHAPTER FIVE

A full week had gone by before Patty Ellsworth was taken off the critical list. Near the end of that week, Dean Warner was forced to submit to an order from Tri-City's new Chief of Staff: completely neglecting his own practice was the young doctor's prerogative, but working in the hospital while physically and emotionally exhausted was not. Dr. Severson was sympathetic, but his directive was firm: Dr. Warner was to get adequate rest, and he would have to trust others to share responsibility for Patty's care.

Near collapse, Dean Warner had no choice but to obey the order. He observed it loosely, nevertheless, and there was no night when he didn't appear once or twice during the still hours of Lillian's shift, stealing into the room silently, standing at Patty's bedside looking at the child with a love so touching that Lillian found it impossible to hold back her tears.

He was in the room on the fourth night following the accident when the deathlike coma that had spread gloom through the hospital finally ended. The doctor was on his way out, following a discouraging visit, when Lillian heard a soft, almost inaudible moan. In the next instant—almost as though she were waking from a normal sleep—Patty opened her eyes.

"Dr. Warner!"

Lillian's joyous summons wasn't necessary. Patty's doctor had heard that small waking sound. He had crossed the room with the swiftness of Mercury.

Patty's eyes, round and blue and pathetically bewildered, were fixed on the doctor's face.

"Patty," he said quietly. "How are you, darling?"

She continued to stare, and for a chilling instant Lillian remembered the blow Patty had suffered on the back of her head as the earth-moving machine had dragged her across the ground. X-rays had offered hope that there was no brain damage, but the long coma had not been a promising symptom.

The grim thought must have raced through Dr. Warner's mind, too, during that terrible silence, but his voice remained calm and steady as he repeated his question: "How are you, Patty? Do you know who this is?"

There was an interminable quiet before Patty nodded her head slightly. And then, with the miraculous impact of an angel choir breaking into the awesome stillness, there was the little-girl voice saying, "Docky . . . Dean."

Dr. Warner choked back a sob of relief and bent to kiss Patty's forehead. Lillian heard him sigh, "Oh, thank God!", but there was a gentle smile on his face when he lifted his head. "You had a bad accident, honey, but Docky Dean's taking good care of you. You're in a nice hospital, and everybody here loves you and is going to help you get all better. Do you understand that, Sweetheart?"

Patty stared at him with complete childhood trust. He was no stranger to her, that was certain. "Docky Dean" was undoubtedly a name she had used as a toddler, before she had been able to pronounce his name and title properly, and it had lingered on as an affectionate nickname they both used. Lillian felt like an intruder at a highly personal reunion of two people who loved each other deeply; she moved away from the bedside, letting Dr. Warner enjoy this moment of triumph in privacy.

He talked to the little girl for another minute or

35

two, explaining to her that she had been hurt, without alarming her, and extracting a promise that she would cooperate with "all the nice doctors and nurses" who were there to help her. He seemed to know exactly the right words to use; words one might consider far beyond the ken of a childless young physician. His "bedside manner" was always good, but right now Dean Warner seemed to possess an instinctive talent for communication that is given only to those who have become close to a child.

Finally, as Patty showed signs of weariness, "Docky Dean" kissed her goodnight, promising to return when she awoke in the morning. He waited until she had closed her eyes once again, watching her with a worshipful expression until he was sure that she was fast asleep before he turned to go. He had already given Lillian a list of instructions. Now, as Lillian moved to replace him at the bedside, he said, "I'd better get out of here." His face lighted up with a sheepish half-smile. "Unless you don't mind seeing a grown doctor bawl like a baby."

"I think you deserve to carry on any way you want to, Doctor," Lillian told him. "You've worked so hard. And I'm so happy for you!"

Dr. Warner reached out, unexpectedly, to press Lillian's hand between his palms. He held it there for a few seconds, letting the warm pressure convey his thoughts. Then, his voice hoarse with emotion, he said, "I won't try to thank you. You know how I feel."

For a tiny microcosm in time, Lillian experienced a wave of hope. Surely there had never been a stronger rapport between two people. They had fought and prayed for a life in this room. Now, although Patty would still need all of their skill—and even more of their tenderness—they had shared a priceless reward for their efforts. This touch of hands was precious to her, yet she longed for a gesture more in keeping with her emotional state. Why couldn't Dr. Warner sweep her into his arms?

Lillian's reply came as her hand was released and the doctor said, more to himself than to her, "I suppose I'd better wait until later in the morning before I phone the Ellsworths." He was looking at his watch. "Three-twenty-five. I'll give them the good news after daylight."

"I can't imagine them minding an encouraging report at *any* hour of the night," Lillian said. Privately, she wondered how Patty's mother had been able to sleep at all during the long ordeal. She had never seen the Ellsworths at the hospital during her shift. Was Carmen Ellsworth more concerned with her beauty-sleep—and did Dr. Warner know this?

He offered a plausible explanation. "Middle-of-the-night calls are always frightening," he said. "No, I'll wait— And speaking of late hours, Miss Bryant . . . after this weekend, I'll want you to take the morning shift. Patty's going to need more attention during her waking hours from now on. There are going to be some painful moments, as you know. We'll be changing dressings, she'll be healing up. I want her to have the best nursing care available. Can you manage?"

Lillian thanked him for the compliment and assured him that she would be glad to make the adjustment to morning hours. Dr. Warner left shortly after that, his step buoyant for the first time since Patty Ellsworth had been admitted to the hospital.

It wasn't until the long night vigil was almost over that a strange thought occurred to Lillian. Patty had been fully conscious. She had recognized her doctor and had understood where she was and why she was there. Her "Docky Dean" had told her how much all the doctors and nurses loved her, how all of them would help her to get well. Yet, in spite of his accurately chosen words, not once had the doctor mentioned Patty's mother and father!

37

More amazing was the fact that Patty had not followed the pattern of every sick or injured child upon regaining consciousness. *Every* child, in Lillian's memory as a nurse, had cried first for Mommy. Patty Ellsworth had gone back to sleep contentedly without either hearing about or asking for her mother. It was as though, for her, the Ellsworths did not exist at all.

CHAPTER SIX

Patty's recovery, though slow and painful, was assured by the time Lillian took over the responsibilities of the seven-to-three shift in Room 406. Her legs remained in a cast, changing of the dressings on her surgically repaired arm were a dreaded ordeal, and even Lillian's most gentle care in moving the tiny patient during her bath or when linens were being changed brought heartrending whimpers: "Oh, it hurts! My chest . . . it *hurts* me!"

Understanding the pain caused by broken ribs on the mend, Lillian would steel herself for the most necessary movements, petting the child's face afterwards, inventing games that would divert Patty's attention from the innumerable hurts and discomforts, grateful that shock had erased the little girl's memory of her dreadful accident. By the end of her first week on the new shift, Lillian had established a warm rapport with Patty—an amazingly courageous and unspoiled child, considering that for five years her every whim had been attended to by a series of maids and governesses. For her tender years, Patty was also surprisingly adult —perhaps even precocious. Her perceptive analysis of staff members, for example, was startling to Lillian, and it was a revelation of Patty's love-starved nature that she divided people into two precise categories; the ones who "really liked" her and the ones who "make it up that they like me."

With an expression so wise that it saddened Lillian,

Patty rated a gushing floor nurse who called her "my precious little sugarplum" as one of the "pretend people." The evaluation was keenly accurate; Miss Rockwell had been known to openly admit her distaste for children. A tough, burly medicine nurse, whose tender loving care was crudely expressed in sentences like, "Let's gulp it down, Kid . . . I haven't got all day!" was placed, by Patty, in the "she really likes me" category. It was a shrewd decision; Norma Kozinski had confided to Lillian that she had been "lighting a candle for that little monkey every morning since they brought her in." There were other judgments, equally correct. The most poignant concerned the people who were closest to Patty.

Every afternoon during the official visiting hours (although, as Patty's parents, they were privileged to spend any hour of the day with her), Howard and Carmen Ellsworth arrived with a flourish, their arms loaded with expensive gifts. Most of the presents were useless to a bedridden child. Invariably, Carmen would look as though she had just stepped from the pages of a fashion magazine, and her husband was no less elegant. Lillian noticed, just before the room was filled with lavish terms of endearment, and the scent of costly perfume, that Patty reluctantly interrupted the game she had been playing with her nurse, and like a stoic old martyr, dutifully waited for her parents' arrival.

It was during one such visit, that Patty tried to embrace her mother, using her uninjured arm in an attempt at a bear hug that entailed great sacrifice; lifting the arm always caused a stabbing pain in the child's rib cage.

It was the sudden, impetuous move of a love-starved little girl. Lillian caught her breath—and even Howard Ellsworth looked shocked—when the beautiful brunette who was Patty's mother jerked away and, with a placating little laugh, exclaimed, "Careful, darling.

40

Mommy's just had her hair done and she has an interview tonight. On a television program. Isn't that nice? Maybe Docky Dean will let you stay up just a teeny-weeny bit later tonight, and then you can see Mommy. Won't that be fun?"

Patty's stunned silence revealed that it wouldn't be fun at all. To have hugged her mother and to have been hugged in return—*that* would have been "fun." Slowly, sounding like an ancient Biblical judge pronouncing sentence, Patty said, "I can't stay up pas' eight-thirty. So I can't see you."

"I'll talk to the doctor," Carmen said. (Her composure was unruffled—was she too insensitive to recognize heartbreak and rejection in her own daughter's eyes?) "You'll see! Mommy will fix it so her poor little baby can stay up way past eight-thirty tonight."

Patty closed her eyes, and Lillian fought an urge to lash out at the stunning woman who looked, suddenly, as though she had been fashioned from plastic. "That's all right," Patty muttered. (Old! She sounded old and weary and frighteningly wise.) "That's okay. I don't want to . . . watch any old television."

There were insincere kisses and promises of more "lovely, lovely presents tomorrow" before Carmen Ellsworth swept out of the room. Her elaborate coiffure was unmarred. Every hair was in place, her artistic makeup looked freshly applied, and not a wrinkle marred the perfection of her exquisitely tailored suit. Yet, in Lillian's eyes, and perhaps in the eyes of her husband and her child, the entrepreneur behind the Carmen Charm School and Modeling Agency looked bedraggled and shabby.

Lillian's guess about Howard Ellsworth's reaction to the cruel snub was correct. The couple had barely left the room before Patty's father was heard accusing, "You shouldn't have done that to the kid! Who the hell cares about your stupid hairdo? The kid needs a *mother!*"

Lillian faked a cough, hoping to drown out the sound of receding voices from the hall; Carmen saying, "A *lot* of people care about the way I look. A few million prospective modeling students, for one thing. This show's a fantastic advertising break for me, Howard, and I've got to look right. Just because *you* don't care anymore. . . ."

Lillian's cough, her deliberately noisy moving of a water pitcher, failed to accomplish its purpose. Or perhaps Patty didn't have to hear the bickering to know what was going on. In that soul-tearing voice that was part little girl, part wizened philospher, she said, "Now they'll have another big fight about me."

Lillian chucked her under the chin. "That's silly, honey. Let's open the rest of these packages. My goodness, you didn't even see what's in this pretty pink box with the. . . ."

"They'll have another big fight," Patty insisted wearily. "About me. And then about her business." There was hardly a trace of emotion in Patty's voice now. Matter-of-factly, as though emotion had long ago been wrung from her, she added, "My mother is pretty famous, I guess. Is your mother famous, Miss Lilly?"

Lillian spared her an explanation of having no Mommy, famous or otherwise. She said "No" and then tried to engage Patty in a guessing contest about the contents of a gift package that had been overlooked in the almost indecent surfeit of presents the Ellsworths had used to assuage their guilt. It was a hopeless effort. Patty refused to guess or even to look at the gift when Lillian unwrapped it. In a roomful of expensive stuffed toys, a plush white teddy bear was easy to ignore.

"Do *you* have a little girl like me?" Patty asked.

Lillian said, "I wish I did, but I don't."

"You could have me. *You* really like me, don't you?"

"I love you very much," Lillian assured her. It was difficult to keep smiling brightly, watching that pretty, pinched little face and seeing the grave expression in the wide blue eyes. She reached out for Patty's hand, and there was an inescapable message in the tight grip with which Patty's fingers encircled her own. "Everybody loves you," Lillian said. "Your Mommy loves you, and your Daddy loves you. . . ." (It was a lie, she knew; a cruelly necessary lie that choked in her throat.) "Dr. Warner loves you. He's doing everything he can to make you feel better, Patty. And Nurse Kozinski, the lady who brings us our medicine, *she* loves you. And that man in the white jacket who makes those funny faces . . . remember the one who made you the paper airplanes, *he* loves. . . ."

"Docky Dean loves me the best of anybody," Patty interrupted. "Could I play with the little mice now?"

"You bet you can." Lillian opened a drawer in the bedstand to bring out a dime-store puzzle toy Dean Warner had brought with him during his morning rounds. Getting the two white plastic mice into a small circular enclosure was a challenge that Patty could easily handle. The simplest effort would be rewarded. Patty had few muscles that could be moved without causing pain, and so, even the successful coordination of her small hands gave her encouragement. Still, Lillian suspected that the child's preference for this unpretentious toy was mainly sentimental.

"This is lots of fun to do," Patty said as she jiggled the window-covered disc back and forth. With exaggerated enthusiasm, she said, "I *love* to play with *this* toy! I'd rather play with my little mice from Docky Dean than *anything*." With a subtlety that would have eluded cynics far older than herself, Patty lowered her voice and said, "This is lots and lots better than watching tel-e-vision. I'd hate to stay up late and hafta watch some dumb old stupid show."

With those words, Patty not only expressed her adoration of a bachelor doctor who was supposedly in love with her mother; she also placed Carmen Ells-

43

worth into that cold never-never land to which she banished the "only pretend people" who professed their liking for her.

Lillian had wept over the brutal injuries to Patty's body. But by comparison with what had been done to the child's psyche, Patty's body was healed and whole.

CHAPTER SEVEN

"Tell him!," Bertha insisted. "Just . . . pin him down and tell him how Patty feels about her parents."

Now that they were working the same shift again, Lillian had resumed her daily lunchtime meetings with Bertha. Typically, the latter had resumed her lecturing services. Today, as they sat at a corner table in Tri-City's pleasant new staff dining room, Lillian looked up from her dessert to warn, "Bertha, I'm here for lunch, not another session of the Risdon Free Counseling Service. It's none of my business how Patty feels about her mother and dad. It's depressing, sure. But I can't see that it's anything I should be writing down on the chart. I'm an R.N., not a child psychiatrist."

Bertha gulped down a swallow of iced tea. "That's for sure. What you don't know about psychology would fill a whole library."

"Oh, I know Patty's recovery would be faster if. . . ."

"I'm not talking about the patient." Bertha sounded exasperated. "I'm talking about the nurse—who just happens to be insanely in love with the doctor—who just happens to think Carmen Ellsworth is some kind of goddess."

"Who gave you that idea?"

"Everybody knows it," Bertha said, her tone secretive. "I've noticed Dr. Warner doesn't talk to Mr. Ellsworth and Mr. Ellsworth doesn't talk to *him*—if that's any clue. But Warner *does* talk to that gorgeous icicle.

You can see where a guy might be infatuated with Mrs. E. But I'll bet if he knew what she's really like. . . ."

"He knows," Lillian sighed. "He's close enough to Patty to see that she feels rejected by her mother. People overlook all kinds of character flaws when they fall in love—this is assuming that he *is* in love with Carmen Ellsworth. In any case, I'm not going to poke my nose into their personal affairs. We learned not to interfere with patients' family matters, remember? Nursing ethics? . . . First semester?"

"The book didn't say anything about standing around for ten years waiting for a guy to notice that you're alive, did it?" Bertha clinked her teaspoon noisily, stirring her tea. She waited until a trio of lab technicians had passed their table before she went on. "Did you see that? Every one of those fellows looked your way. If I was everybody's idea of The Perfect Irish Beauty . . ."

Lillian laughed. "Please, not *that* again!"

"If I had a perfect figure and shiny black hair and lavender-blue eyes and long lashes that don't need mascara and. . . ."

"You'd be out on the town every night with one of those three jokers from the lab," Lillian finished. "It just happens that I don't want to go out with anyone else."

"No, you'd rather be a sulking martyr. Waste your life brooding. Nursing a hopeless case." Bertha shrugged her bony shoulders. "Okay. Wallow in rejection. Wait'll the Ellsworths get their divorce and then you can blubber in your lonely little room while your hero makes wedding plans with Carmen."

There was no arguing with Bertha: not only because she held fixed, inflexible opinions, but because most of what she said was usually true. "I won't stay around for that," Lillian predicted. "But I'm not going to try to compete with a woman who gives lessons in how to charm males. And what I *definitely* am not going to do is try to undermine a . . . romance that doesn't concern me. Dr. Warner's a big boy. If he wants to involve himself with a woman who. . . ." She stopped, determined not to express her opinion of Carmen Ellsworth again. "So maybe it's a hopeless, one-sided case. It's the way it is, that's all." A leaden, sinking feeling came over her. "Let's not talk about it, hey, Bertie?"

Bertha grinned. "Talk about *my* scintillating love life for a change? Want a progress report on Vernon?"

Lillian managed a smile. "Fine. You said he held your hand during the movie last night."

"Yeah, isn't that wild? Honestly, you'd think this was the Victorian age." Bertha's grin faded and she was suddenly quiet and serious. After a long pause, she said, "Maybe it's never going to be one of those grand passions you see in the movies, Lil, but . . . I don't know. At my age, you start getting willing to settle for . . . well, just being at ease with a man. Old-shoe comfortable."

"Now you sound like you're ready for a rocking chair," Lillian chided.

"That's not what I mean. Vernon's sort of . . . square and conservative. But he's a kind person, and he's been coming around a lot longer than any man I've ever known. Face it, I'm no ravishing young beauty. And there's all kinds of love, you know. The nice, relaxing type where two people know they can . . . trust each other and enjoy simple things together. Maybe you think Vernon isn't much, but. . . ."

"Don't apologize for him," Lillian said softly. "Most of all, don't apologize for the way you feel about him." She looked directly into Bertha's lovable, yet far-from-glamorous face, seeing—beyond the scraggly features—an inner beauty that the Carmens of the world could very well envy. "I think he'd be lucky to have you as his wife. Vernon's one of the good guys, and that's what counts. Those dashing, handsome characters women are supposed to fall in love with only exist in confession magazines. The Real McCoy is somebody you can *live* with. Like you said . . . someone you can trust over the years, and . . ."

Bertha made a giggling sound. "Hey, I haven't got Vernon to *that* stage yet." She was pensive for a moment. "He's slow. Vernon doesn't jump into things." Bertha lifted her head, and in the shining green eyes Lillian saw that all the talk about "old-shoe comfort" was nothing more than a self-conscious evasion. Bertha was really in love; genuinely and deeply in love. And it was only because she had waited and despaired for so many years that she was reluctant to make the admission now. Failure would be painful enough without someone else feeling sorry for her. Bertha made a joke of it. "Ah, well. Don't hold your breath, but in a few months Vernon might advance to the chaste-kiss-on-the-forehead stage. I never believe in rushing these mad, impetuous types. He's probably all wracked up with guilt over that hand-holding bit."

They made small talk as they finished their lunch, each enclosed in her own private thought-chamber, Lilliam glumly facing a fact that she had avoided far too long: Dean Warner had been given plenty of opportunity to recognize her as something more than a dedicated nurse. Bertha was right; only a masochist would go on waiting for something that wasn't ever going to happen. It would be wonderful if love could be turned off like a light switch—if this terrible aching could be dispelled by logic (*he doesn't love me, he's never going to love me, forget him*).

But it wasn't that simple, Lillian knew. Maybe the only solution lay in going somewhere—anywhere—where she would never see Dean Warner again. Everyone said that time was a great healer. But what if you didn't *want* to be healed?

CHAPTER EIGHT

Arizona's dry summer heat had worn on into early August, and it seemed to Lillian that she had never known any other life, never attended any patient but Patty Ellsworth.

Patty's casts had been removed. The orthopedic doctors had given hope that the child would one day walk again, and there were further triumphs to celebrate in Room 406: Patty's first wheelchair ride around the hospital's specimen ·cactus garden, the morning when she was able to lift both arms over her head, the day when she was able to turn over in bed unassisted without wincing in pain.

These were physical changes in the little girl Lillian had learned to love, and each mark of progress was gratefully observed. But there were no other changes. Patty waited for no visits except those of her doctor. Lillian waited for Dean Warner's visits, too, suffering through the aggravating hypocrisies of Patty's unfailingly glamorous mother. Howard Ellsworth's appearances were less frequent now. He was busy, Patty was told, with a very important project. Patty was indifferent. She had been raised with such "very important projects," resigning herself to the fact that whatever it was that occupied her parents apart from her came first. If she had cried and begged them to come more often, the damage might not have seemed so severe, Lillian thought. It was Patty's indifference to the two people who should have been her world that was so shocking. At age five, she was a hard-bitten realist.

More realistic than I am, Lillian reflected. More mature, more adult. Waiting for the sound of Dean Warner's footsteps in the corridor outside was childish. The breathless feeling when he was present in the room—wasn't this worthy of a starry-eyed adolescent?

Trying to resign herself to being unwanted, just as her small patient had resigned herself, Lillian was unprepared for an invitation that Dean Warner issued one afternoon as casually as if he had been referring to the weather.

"Nice to finally be able to take a day off," he said. They were walking toward the charge desk at the end of Lillian's shift. "I know you wouldn't have left Patty with any other nurse a few weeks ago. Right?"

"I hate to leave her now," Lillian told him. "Even for a day. I won't know what to do with myself tomorrow, it's been so long since I had a day to myself."

"Wouldn't want to go back to the reservation?"

"Go back to . . . ?"

Dr. Warner smiled. "I have a patient to see tomorrow morning at an Indian reservation about two hours' drive out of town. And I've promised to deliver some drugs to the resident doctor there. Would you like a look at the desert at the crack of dawn? I can't promise any more than a cool, beautiful ride around sunrise and . . . probably a sweltering drive home around noon."

As Lillian told Bertha that evening, she would have accepted an invitation to visit a nest of Gila monsters. As far as her romantic illusions were concerned, the end result would have been identical.

The drive through the morning freshness was exhilarating, the air bracing, Dean Warner's knowledge of local flora and fauna impressive. He had stopped for Lillian before daylight, anxious to complete his errand before the afternoon sun blistered the desert, and, as dawn brought a dazzling pink glow to the vast stretches bisected by a highway which was theirs alone, Lillian's heart pounded with the thrill of romantic adventure. She had not dared to dream that they would one day be together in this scene of incredible peace and beauty. Surely Dean Warner had known—and perhaps hoped for—the effect that this strangely lovely picture would have upon her. Long spikes of ocotillo cactus reached like fingers to point out the rose tinted sky. Grotesque formations of cholla and an occasional pipe organ cactus stood silhouetted against the rising sun, in an unfamiliar, otherworldly landscape. Only once was the serenity disturbed when a pair of vultures swooped down to roost on the trembling branches of a lone palo verde tree. All else was stillness.

Lillian waited for the word, the gesture, that would break the formal wall that separated her from the man at her side. It didn't materialize. The doctor was an agreeable host, concerned about Lillian's comfort and enjoyment—but that was all. At the small clinic on the reservation, he introduced her to Indian friends as the "finest nurse on the Tri-City staff." He led her on a capsule tour of the humble medical facility and nearby school. He stood by, smiling his approval as a pair of shy fifth-graders told Lillian that they hoped to be nurses some day, and while he visited his patient he saw to it that Lillian was not left alone. She was treated to a half-hour visit with a family of Indian potters, watching art works emerge under red bronzed fingers that had not forgotten ancient skills. Her host then bought a beautifully decorated vase for Lillian as a memento.

That was it. The drive back to Phoenix was an almost wordless melancholy experience. While having lunch at a smart restaurant in Scottsdale—during which the doctor asked to be called by his first name and made a rather stiff speech thanking Lillian for her devotion to his little patient—Lillian made her final

51

decision. To go on longing for the impossible was a cruel joke. There was still a responsibility to Patty; the child was on her way to recovery, but she faced many trials and probably many disappointments before she could be abandoned by a nurse on whom she leaned emotionally as well as physically. But as soon as Patty was ready to be released, Lillian promised herself an escape from this tormenting situation. Nurses were in demand everywhere; somewhere, anywhere, she would free herself of this pointless misery.

They shook hands at Lillian's doorstep, and, for a moment, as Dean remarked that the pool looked tempting, Lillian thought of inviting him to stay for a dip—perhaps even to linger on for a home-cooked dinner. (How short-lived was that resolution to try to forget this man!) The doctor squelched that idea before it was suggested, saying, "Patty's going to wonder what's keeping me. I'll see you in the morning, Lillian. Thanks for keeping me company. It's a rather dull drive when you go it alone."

Lillian could have expanded on that sentence. "Going it alone" was worse than dull; it could be pure anguish. But there was nothing she could properly say except to thank the doctor in return, after which she hurried to the sanctuary of her room. Bertha was still at the hospital, fortunately, and tears would go unseen.

CHAPTER NINE

Besides Dean Warner, there were two other male visitors who called on Patty Ellsworth almost daily.

Lillian was not surprised by Vernon Jessup's brief visits. As an administrator who liked to observe Tri-City's functioning at first hand, he was a frequent sight in the wards, often dropping in to check on the kitchen or laundry room personnel unannounced, or chatting with lower-echelon staff members instead of depending on reports from department heads for his information. True, he didn't pay daily visits to the rooms of other patients, but Patty had become something of a hospital pet; off-duty nurses from other floors came to amuse her, one of the cleaning women had made a project of teaching Patty to knit, and a Negro college student who worked part-time in the staff dining room had presented her with a bowl of goldfish. Because her injuries had been so severe and because she was so appreciative of attention, Patty had gathered a veritable fan club of hospital employees around her. It was not unusual that Vernon Jessup made it a point to visit Room 406 every afternoon at around two.

Having discovered that he could not interest a five-year-old girl in his hobby of stamp collecting, Vernon Jessup had quickly run out of ideas with which to capture Patty's interest. Now, usually, he exchanged a few awkward inanities with the child and then stood around fidgetting for a few more minutes before mumbling an excuse about having important duties elsewhere. Lillian had no more to say to him than she did on the twice-weekly occasions when he came to gorge himself on one of Bertha's dinners at the apartment. She sympathized with Vernon's lack of ease (a strange attribute in a man whose job depended upon dealing with people) and, when he lingered in the room too long, found herself growing uncomfortable, dredging her mind for something to say to him.

"Mr. Jessup's a sort of in-the-middle man," Patty decided. "He sort of does like me but not 'specially lots—like the man who gave me my fishies, or Docky Dean."

"Oh, I'm sure Mr. Jessup is fond of you," Lillian said. "He's a busy man, in charge of this whole big hospital. He wouldn't come to see the same little girl every single day if he didn't think she was very, very nice."

"Busy people are mostly sort of in-the-middle," Patty said. She didn't elaborate, and Lillian accepted this as one of the child's fixed philosophies; there were undoubtedly ramifications that would lead them into personal waters if an explanation were demanded. For example, Patty's father was known to be an extremely busy man, too. And he was as inept in establishing a rapport with Patty as was the bachelor from Administration.

It was Howard Ellsworth who was the other daily visitor. Since Patty had been taken off the critical list her father had taken to visiting her alone, usually at a time when Dean Warner was busy at his office. Happily for Lillian, his wife did her visiting during Patty's five-thirty dinner hour—on another nurse's shift.

Mr. Ellsworth was spared the effort of trying to make conversation with his daughter one morning when his visit coincided with Patty's wheelchair excursion to the hospital garden. A seven-year-old girl recovering from orthopedic surgery occupied another wheelchair, providing welcome juvenile company for

Patty and allowing her elderly nurse to catch up on her reading.

Leaving the children to their private little-girl prattle, Lillian sat on a stone bench several yards away. Patty's father settled himself beside her, an imposing figure who fulfilled all the Hollywood requirements for the stereotype of the big wealthy Western businessman. Yet Lillian noticed that his hands were those of a laborer—large and rough, in spite of an expert manicure and two costly rings that enhanced his fingers.

"Wonderful to see Patty giggling . . . sitting out here in the sun with another little kid." Howard Ellsworth sighed, his workman's hands flexing nervously. "That's always been a problem. We live in this condominium I built. Last word in luxury, but most young couples can't afford to live at Ellsworth Manor. I never thought about it before, but Patty's always been surrounded by adults. I guess . . . not that I know much about kids, but . . . it's great she's got somebody closer to her own age to play with."

Lillian agreed. "When I told her there'd be another little girl out here today she was terribly excited. We're going to try to let her spend as much time with Dorothy as possible. As long as they're both here."

"I don't suppose Patty will be here too much longer?"

"I can't see why she should be," Lillian said. "Has Dr. Warner said anything to you about. . . ."

Mr. Ellsworth's rugged face clouded, as though the question embarrassed him. "I haven't heard. Maybe my wife knows. She hasn't said anything."

"It shouldn't be too long," Lillian assured him. "She'll need nursing care for awhile, but I think she's past the sort of problems that require hospital care."

"They . . . I mean, doctors usually try to get a patient home as soon as possible, don't they?" Patty's father smoothed his rust-colored hair from his broad forehead, his manner one of controlled nervousness.

"I've heard people recover faster if their morale is good."

"That's right. Sometimes a homesick patient doesn't make any progress at all. *Patty's* been. . . ." Lillian fumbled for a way out of the sentence she had started. ". . . She's been wonderfully cooperative."

"What you mean," Howard said, "is that she isn't anxious to go home."

"I didn't mean that!"

"It's true." There was the heavy sound of self-condemnation in the man's voice. "Why should she look forward to coming home? To what? A roomful of toys? She's got that here. A ritzy building full of retired ranchers? I didn't build the Manor for kids, Miss Bryant. There's a pool, but it's mostly for show. And there's no playground. No place for a kid to run around or ride a bike . . . whatever it is little girls like to do. I've been thinking about that. Y'know, until Patty got hurt, I never gave it any thought at all."

Lillian searched for a comment that wouldn't be construed as criticism. "Well, since you're a contractor, that shouldn't be too hard to change. Maybe you'll build a place out in the country. I always dreamed about having a place with room for a playhouse and a big vegetable garden and trees. When I was Patty's age, my idea of heaven was a playhouse. A place where my friends could come, but no adults. Just kids and cats and dogs."

Howard Ellsworth smiled, but the edge of melancholy stayed in his voice. "Never got that?"

"Oh, no. Matter of fact, I never had a room of my own until I came out here to work. I was always under somebody's watchful eye. Critical adults, usually."

"No brothers and sisters?"

It would have sounded melodramatic to tell him that she had been a lonely orphan. Lillian shook her head. "Nope. So I know how much Patty's enjoying herself over there. Look at her! I've never seen her so happy."

56

There was no reply, but Lillian noticed that Patty's father was staring at the child, a solemn expression resting like a shadow over his features.

"If you don't like living way out in the country, I'll bet Patty would love being in a neighborhood—one of the developments around here where you can't get past the driveways for all the bicycles and scooters. I think . . . didn't someone tell me you've built several of the new tracts in the area?"

"Carmen . . . my wife wouldn't live in a tract. She likes the convenience, the elegance of the place we're in now. Spent a fortune having it decorated the way she wants it. You know—a woman with Carmen's taste. We entertain a lot—business reasons. And the place is convenient to my office—to my wife's studio." There was a long pause, as though Mr. Ellsworth had run out of justifications and found himself squarely faced with a wall of guilt. "It's not right for Patty, though. Not just the apartment—everything. The maids, the kid just about getting adjusted to one old battle-ax and Carmen firing her because she didn't peel the damned salad tomatoes. Like, she didn't come up the hard way, the way I did. You talk about wanting a room of your own when you were young! I lived in a shack outside Tucson . . . nine kids, the folks, a couple of arthritic aunts and a grandfather who was still hitting the bottle at ninety. Peeling the tomatoes, for Pete's sake! We were lucky if we saw anything on the table besides pinto beans. And don't kid yourself— Carmen's folks didn't have *that*. And they still wouldn't, if I didn't remind my wife to send them a check once a month. How do you figure a woman like that, Miss Bryant? *Charm*. She teaches other females how to have *charm!* It turns my gut!"

Embarrassed by the revealing tirade, Lillian made an attempt to change the subject. "Now, there's charm for you! Look at those girls . . . I'll swear they're trying to see which one's hair is longer—or is it blonder? I washed Patty's this morning and she was. . . ."

"That's the amazing thing about you medical people," Patty's father cut in. "You don't want to hear gossip, you don't care about putting blame on others. Just helping other people. You take that so much for granted."

"That's our job," Lillian protested.

"I know, but you . . . I don't know. You'd have to live with a person who lives only for herself . . . *strictly* for herself . . . and then you'd know what I mean. My mother was like you. I've watched you around Patty, so don't tell me you only do what you're getting paid for. You get a kick out of doing little things that'll make the kid happy. Little things Carmen wouldn't even think of. Like rearranging her plate that one time to make the vegetables look like a—what the heck was it?—a rabbit face, or whatever. Don't tell me they hired you to do that."

"Patty's a little girl and she's had a bad break," Lillian said. "Anything any of us here can do to make her happy. . . ."

Mr. Ellsworth slapped his knee with one of his big hands. *"There's* a good example! That's exactly what I mean! The way you put that: 'Patty's had a bad break.' You didn't bring up all the suffering. You didn't remind me the kid won't ever be able to wear a low cut dress because she'll have scars on her shoulders, or . . . that she may not ever walk right."

Lillian turned to stare at Mr. Ellsworth, alarmed by his agonized tone. "Why should I mention anything as unpleasant as that, Mr. Ellsworth? We don't dwell on the past. We all know it's been rough on Patty, but it was painful for you, too. I wouldn't. . . ."

"You wouldn't remind me that it was my fault," he cried. Then, conscious of the children nearby, Howard Ellsworth lowered his voice. "Look—look, I'm not going to deny I was to blame. I put that kid through a hell on earth, but don't think I don't know it. I'm not used to kids. I've been working so hard . . . one thing on my mind and nothing else. Coming up from the bottom. Big bank account, big cars, beautiful wife. In my line, you've got to be on the ball just to stay even with the board, let alone get ahead. So, that day, I was talking to my foreman on the job and I forgot about Patty. We had earth-moving equipment going all over the project and I forgot she was there. I didn't mean. . . ."

"Mr. Ellsworth, stop that!" Lillian's sharp warning ended the rising note of hysteria that had crept into the man's voice. Patty had turned to look back at them, and Lillian smiled her assurance that all was well. More subdued herself, she said, "Everyone knows it was an accident, Mr. Ellsworth. No one blames you, and you've got to stop blaming yourself. It isn't good for *you* . . . and it isn't going to be good for Patty if she hears you raking yourself over the coals for something that can't be helped now! It won't even be good for Patty if you try to overcompensate. It's not my business, but she doesn't need one more expensive toy. She's gotten more pleasure from a fifty-cent bowl of goldfish than. . . ."

"I know, I *know!*" The big man's hands rubbed across his face and then rested disconsolately in his lap. "If it wasn't for people like you, I'd go crazy thinking about it. You and Dean . . . Dr. Warner. If anybody worked to save the kid's life, the two of you . . . my God, you ought to be the first ones reminding me about who's to blame. But he hasn't said a word. Not one word! And you . . . here *you* are, telling me I shouldn't be all wracked up with guilt."

"We aren't monsters, Mr. Ellsworth! We're human. We make mistakes. In a hospital . . . you can't begin to imagine the possibilities for error, or the torture a doctor has to endure when he knows he's going to lose a patient. When he can't think of one more thing to do, and maybe somewhere in the treatment he made a wrong judgment—guessed wrong, when doing something else might have meant the difference between life and death. People who live with something like this day after day . . . people who can't afford to fall apart because of guilt. . . ." Lillian followed a mindless impulse, reaching out to pat Howard Ellsworth's forearm. "They're the last people on earth to rub in the blame for an accident."

Lillian regretted her friendly gesture in almost the same second that she made it. Mr. Ellsworth was looking at her with gratitude, but there was something more reflected in his eyes—a warmly personal look that left Lillian flustered.

It was the beginning of a new phase in Lillian's relationship with a man desperately in need of understanding. Until then, Mr. Ellsworth had been only the father of her patient; after that conversation in the garden, he insisted on being recognized as a friend. It was one of those situations against which the textbooks on nursing ethics warned neophyte angels of mercy. Yet didn't the books teach that a patient's next of kin were also in need of sympathy? Out of a natural wellspring of kindness for unhappy people, Lillian poured out the gentle affection Howard needed. It occurred to her only briefly—and Lillian dismissed the thought—that anyone who was dependent upon Carmen Ellsworth for love had a need for more than simple friendship.

CHAPTER TEN

"It's perfectly innocent," Lillian argued from her bedroom. Beyond the open door, she could see Bertha in her own room, going through the ritual of selecting a dress to wear during tonight's "at-home date" with Vernon Jessup. "There's absolutely nothing wrong with having dinner with someone who wants to do a little something to show his appreciation. That's all there's to it, Bertha."

"Tell him to send you a box of chocolates," Bertha yelled across the hall. "Maybe a bunch of roses with a thank-you card attached. That's what other married men do when they want to thank a nurse. Candy or flowers. Not dinner in some fancy rendezvous without the wife. . . ."

"Mrs. Ellsworth knows all about it," Lillian cried. "She'd have come, too, except that she has a style-show rehearsal tonight."

Bertha crossed the hall to stand in the open doorway. "Is *that* what he told you? Boy, are you naive! Wait'll he starts pouring on the champagne and telling you his wife doesn't understand him."

Lillian smoothed her nylons and slipped into a new pair of brightly colored pumps. "These don't make me look too much like an Easter egg, do they?"

"Okay, ignore me! I'm telling you the guy's married, he's not getting along with his wife, and he knows a big-hearted hayseed when he sees one."

Lillian stood up, laughing. "I'm not just fresh in from the farm, Bertie. I'm. . . ."

"They've got hayseeds in the big cities, too," Bertha grumbled. "Look, if Mrs. Ellsworth *doesn't* know you're going out with her husband, you're asking for big trouble—personal *and* professional. Trouble, period. If she knows and doesn't give a damn—which, come to think of it, sounds like a good bet, then you're practically inviting a pass. What you should have said when Mr. Ellsworth asked for a date, was. . . ."

"He didn't ask for a date!" Lillian shouted. Bertha's moralistic lecture was beginning to get on her nerves. "I happened to mention that beautiful new adobe shopping center they've just finished over on Coronado Street, and it turned out that it was one of Howard's projects. So. . . ."

"I know. So he offered you a private guided tour of all the fountains and the central plaza with the lava rock and waterfall and. . . ."

"Is there anything wrong with that? *Yes!* That's *exactly* what we're going to do during this big clandestine date. And then have dinner at the new El Adobe restaurant next to the plaza. Howard built that, too, and he wants me to see the decor. Big deal!"

Bertha made a loud, derisive noise. "That beats the line about going up to see a guy's etchings!"

"It's a public place. It'll be full of people Howard Ellsworth knows." Lillian picked up her handbag from the dresser, and in a explosive burst of anger slammed it down on her bed. "Why do I have to stand here justifying a silly little dinner with a . . . a guilt-ridden father? Maybe you've been thinking about how to trap a man for so long that you can't think any other way. You've got to take a perfectly wholesome gesture of appreciation and twist it into something sinister . . . something shoddy! And I can do without all your advice, too! Calling *me* naive, when you've got that boring free-loader coming around again tonight to mootch another meal. When did you become such an expert on male intentions? How do *you* rate, telling me I shouldn't . . ."

Lillian's rage and her bitter words came to an abrupt halt. Bertha was no longer listening. She had made a choking sound, that was both a sob and a cry of indignation, and she had left the doorway. Lillian heard the door to Bertha's bedroom slam. The jarring noise was followed by a click that told her the door had been locked from the inside.

What had possessed her to hurl out the most pain-inflicting words imaginable? Bertha was crying—there was no sound from the next room, but there was no doubt in Lillian's mind that her friend was weeping bitter tears. What a rotten way to release one's tensions! What an outlet for frustration—lashing out at a woman who already viewed herself as pitifully unattractive, throwing the cruelest barb imaginable at a friend who needed encouragement, not a crushing blow to her ego.

Lillian walked across the hall and turned the doorknob. "Bertha? I'm sorry. I'm really sorry."

There was no response. "I got mad because I know you're perfectly right. I shouldn't have accepted this date. I just wasn't thinking."

Bertha remained silent behind her locked door.

"Did you hear me, Bertie? I apologize. We all say things we don't mean when we're angry. I've been so miserable . . . you know how misery loves company." Lillian reached out for a convincing argument. "I'm just jealous. You've got someone who really cares for you. All I've got is a stupid daydream. Come on, Bert. Vernon's going to be here any minute. Let's forget I said anything—please?"

There were no words with which to repair the damage. Bertha was still closeted in her room when Howard Ellsworth came for Lillian, and Howard's Cadillac was pulling away from the curb as Vernon Jessup arrived. It wasn't going to be the best of evenings, Lillian thought glumly. Not that Bertha wouldn't recover and not that Bertha wouldn't forgive her; it was Bertha's nature to forgive. Still, it was one of those times that one wished could be erased completely and started again all over.

Bertha's predictions—at least the one about free-flowing champagne—proved accurate. In the candle-lit El Adobe dining room, with its dark-panelled walls and richly carpeted floor, the champagne was a natural complement to the elegance and intimate atmosphere.

Besides, Lillian's self-incrimination had turned to annoyance and, finally, to indifference. Bertha had asked for it, hadn't she? All those nasty implications, for heaven's sake! And then dramatizing herself, acting like a hammy adolescent by locking herself up in her room. She had probably snapped to attention the instant Vernon Jessup's finger touched the doorbell. Ole Bertie was doubtless knocking herself out at this very minute, waiting on that beefy dullard and enjoying herself thoroughly. Why should I let a little argument spoil an otherwise pleasant dinner? Lillian asked herself. She decided that she wouldn't. The lobster was delicious. She smiled as Howard refilled her champagne glass.

He had filled an uncounted number of champagne glasses, they had danced at the Desert Sky Room downtown, and Lillian had stopped withdrawing her hand from Howard's touch before the evening ended. When the Cadillac had purred to a stop in front of Lillian's apartment court, it was the most natural thing in the world for Howard's arm to fall lightly around her shoulders after he had cut off the ignition.

"I don't know when I've had a more wonderful evening," he said quietly.

Lillian felt a mixture of exhilaration and contentment. Her head snuggled easily against Howard's chest. Why not? He had told her that he and his wife had been on the verge of divorce months before Patty's accident. Only that tragic occurrence had held them together, but they were both agreed that their marriage was a failure. "I'm going to move into a place of my own next week," he had said. "I'll be alone, but that'll be better than living with a woman who doesn't know what love is. Can't even . . . when she makes a conscious effort . . . can't even generate any love for her own child."

Nothing had been said about the effect of such a move on Patty; likely, Patty wouldn't care one way or the other. Then, too, Lillian preferred not to think about it. It was easier, now, to feel close to someone who appreciated her as a woman and not just as a starched white uniform and cap that represented efficiency.

"You're so completely different." Howard's voice was deep and richly masculine, softened by an unpretentious, friendly Western drawl. He had the strength of a man who had known what it means to work hard for a living; as his arm tightened around her, Lillian responded to the pull of male strength and protectiveness. "I don't want you to misunderstand this, Lillian. I'm not in any position to . . . offer you anything right now. Fact is, I'm going to need somebody to lean on in the months ahead. Breaking up even a loveless marriage is a bad experience. It would mean a lot to have. . . ." Howard smiled. "What's the word for it?"

"Moral support?"

"Let's call it that," Howard murmured. He drew Lillian into his arms and kissed her.

It was a dreamlike experience, vague and yet intensely exciting. She had forgotten how long it had been since warm lips had closed over hers, and she had been held closely like this. Lillian gave herself to the rapturous mood, yet a portion of her mind (that portion that was not experiencing a tingly, bubbling sensation) viewed the scene objectively, reminding her that this man was a stranger, a *married* stranger—And wasn't she in love with someone else? Yes, but someone who had never kissed her and probably never would, and this was an attractive man who had asked for her help, a man who . . . *But wasn't she in love with someone else?*

Howard had lifted his face from hers, and now he was breathing heavily, saying "I'm crazy about you, honey. You're everything I've always wanted." In some remote, darkened corner of her consciousness, Lillian heard the resonant voice adding, "You're everything I wanted Carmen to be."

Carmen. Patty's mother. This stranger's *wife!* The name struck at Lillian's awareness like an electrical charge. Suddenly the pleasant floating sensation, the easy rapport, was shattered, and she was struggling to free herself. Senseless. Lillian heard herself crying, "I don't know what I'm doing. Let me go."

Howard released her from his embrace. She heard him repeating "I'm sorry . . . I'm sorry if I upset you" just the way she had repeated her apology to Bertha, sounding somewhat alarmed and genuinely contrite. "I shouldn't have done that, Honey. I didn't mean to. . . ."

She was crying. Sitting beside an embarassed, plainly miserable man who undoubtedly wished that he, too, were elsewhere. Lillian managed, somehow, to thank him for dinner and to assure him that they were still friends, though he must have sensed that she would not want to see him again. Nevertheless, Howard said, "I'm not going to forget you, Lillian. When I'm free, you'll hear from me again."

Walking to her door, Lillian had to make a strong effort to walk without weaving back and forth. It was only part of the degradation that wracked her insides. About the only thing for which she could be grateful was the fact that Vernon Jessup's car had not been parked outside, and that Bertha was probably asleep; facing herself was enough of an ordeal without being seen in this state by others.

CHAPTER ELEVEN

Predictably, when Bertha Risdon made an about-face three days later, she insisted that she didn't want to hear any more apologies. As Lillian drove toward the hospital that morning, her friend was in an exuberant mood that contrasted strongly with her chilly sulking during the past few days. "Let's not talk about it," Bertha insisted.

The ice had finally been broken during breakfast, and Bertha had accepted the usual ride in Lillian's car instead of walking to the bus stop. Lillian relaxed behind the wheel. "I just wanted you to know I didn't mean any of those ugly. . . ."

"I *said* let's forget it." Bertha snapped open a compact and inspected her newly bleached hair. She had come home the evening before with a platinum job that glittered now in the morning light. "I was feeling pretty depressed the other night. I had to take it out on somebody, and you were the handiest target." Bertha nodded approval at her reflection and closed the compact. "I knew darned well you weren't rushing into a life of sin with a married man. Just for the record, did you have a nice evening?"

"So-so. Good lobster. You know how crazy I am about lobster." Lillian turned the car into the street leading toward Tri-City Hospital. She had sounded properly noncommittal. There would be no need now

68

to confess that she had, indeed, behaved like a naive "hayseed," that champagne and sympathy had distorted her judgment, and that she realized any reasonably understanding woman would have brought out the same emotional response from Howard Ellsworth. Nor was it necessary to tell Bertha that Patty's father was discreetly staying away from the hospital between seven and three. Bertha had other matters on her mind. "Yeah, well, as I said, I'd been feeling kind of down in the dumps about this whole bit with Vernon," Bertha said. "When I get mad at myself, I usually start picking somebody else apart."

"Like the rest of us," Lillian assured her. "I lashed out at you for exactly the same reason."

"Sure. Anyway, I was feeling low because it looked like I was getting exactly nowhere with Vernon. I wasn't good company that evening, so he went home early and I felt even worse than ever."

"You're in pretty good spirits this morning," Lillian observed.

"Well, I decided it was high time I quit fooling around and pinned Mr. Jessup down. Either he's serious or he can stop wasting my time, you know? At my age, you haven't got all the time in the world."

They had passed the ambulance ramp, and Lillian turned into the employees' parking lot. "Have you given him an ultimatum, Bertie? Set a time limit?"

"You think I'm *that* anxious to send Vernon running for the hills?" Bertha paused. "No-o-o, I just have a hunch he's going to get down to cases very, very soon. He's been talking about how he hates eating in restaurants and having to worry about getting his shirts starched properly. When he got off on that the other night, I played it so cool, you wouldn't have believed it. I casually mentioned something about . . . why didn't he hire a housekeeper, and that got him into a speech about how hired help and living in an apart-ment-hotel wasn't the same as having a real home of your own. And how, as you got older, it was important to have someone else around." Bertha giggled self-con-sciously, sounding a trifle too girlish for comfort. "That may not sound romantic to you, baby, but com-ing from Vernon Jessup, it's almost an impassioned proposal."

"Maybe he's afraid you'll turn him down," Lillian said. "Maybe all he needs is a little nudge."

"That's what I figured," Bertha agreed. "So, he's coming to dinner tonight, and this kid hasn't missed an angle. You haven't seen my new outfit yet. Vernon likes pink, and I mean this dress is really *pink!* You're sure you like my hair this color? It doesn't make my face look. . . ."

"It's very pretty," Lillian told her.

They got out of the car and started walking toward one of the hospital's rear doors.

"In case he isn't flipped by my platinum tresses *or* that gorgeous pink job that set me back thirty-nine ninety-five, I've got a whole battery of guns lined up. Two steaks about *yea* thick, a couple of new albums for background music, some French perfume—and we won't talk about what I paid for *that*—the whole works, Lilly. And if the dinner and the music *and* the glamour girl bit all fail, I've still got one *more* bomb to drop."

Lillian paused at the hospital door. "Oh?"

"I'm going to put my arms around *him* and tell Vernon the truth. I'm in love with him—bam—just like that. If he still looks at his watch at ten o'clock and reminds me that we both have to be up early the next morning, I'll give up. But I don't think he's going to do *that*. From the noises he's been making. . . ." Bertha sighed and pulled open the door. "I think all he needs is that little nudge you mentioned. So do me a favor tonight, okay, pal?"

"Get lost?"

"I wasn't planning to put it that crudely, but you've got the idea."

They were both laughing as they approached the nurses' station, where Bertha had the supreme pleasure of having her new silvery coiffure admired by the head nurse, an orderly, and two wildly enthusiastic aides. Lillian had never seen her happier or more effervescent. Not even Vernon Jessup could miss seeing the love glow that lighted her thin face. Hopefully, the glow would reflect from his own face before this day was ended.

There was activity in Room 406 this morning. The last of Patty's casts had been removed, there had been a wheelchair trip to the X-ray room, and now, after a long suspenseful wait, Dean Warner and Dr. Berens, who headed Tri-City's Orthopedic department, came into the room radiating pleasure. Lillian studied their expressions for a moment and then said, "I don't have to ask what the pictures showed, Doctors. You've got the report written all over your faces."

Dr. Berens laughed. "I've heard you nurses have that face-reading science down pat. Well, you're right, Miss Bryant. We got good, clear pictures and a good, clean mind. Beautiful."

They didn't go into details—with Patty listening—but Lillian understood the verdict. Her patient would walk normally. Her progress from wheelchair to crutches might be slow, but the last fear of permanent crippling had been eliminated.

Dean had walked over to Patty's side, probably surprising her with the fervency of his embrace. "We're out of the woods, little one," he said. "We're out of the woods."

Patty looked to her nurse for an explanation. "Your doctor means you're just about all well now, honey."

"Can we go in the woods?" Patty asked. "To see the bears and make a picnic?"

Dr. Berens, a graying, gaunt man who usually looked as though he had just attended his best friend's funeral, laughed again. "This certainly calls for some sort of celebration. I'm just as pleased as can be. And, looking back, not a little surprised."

Lillian nodded, knowing what he meant; there had only been one doctor at Tri-City who had believed that Patty's recovery would be complete. Dean Warner was grateful, but he was not surprised; and, seeing him now with his little patient—who was, somehow, more than just a patient—was seeing a man whose faith had been fully rewarded.

"I don't know about a picnic in the woods," Dr. Berens said, "but you'll be going home soon, Patty. That should be just as good."

He expected the customary reaction: a whoop of joy, or a childish, "Oh, boy!" Patty only looked at him gravely. "Do I hafta?" she asked.

It was the orthopedic doctor's turn to look puzzled. "You want to go home, don't you, dear?"

Patty wrapped her arms around Dean Warner's forearm, gripping him tightly as though she expected him to run away if she let him go. "I want to stay here," she said. "I like to be right here."

Apparently Dr. Warner had no desire to let anyone else know that Patty's home life left something to be desired. "The whole staff's been spoiling our little gal, I'm afraid. Patty's gotten to be queen bee here at the hospital."

Dr. Berens mumbled something about Patty proba-

72

bly getting all the ice cream she could eat, offering that as an explanation. But when he left the room shortly afterward, he was still bewildered. Hospitalized children *always* wanted to go home. Even the poorest youngsters in the charity clinic were willing to forego all that ice cream to return to meager fare in the hovels they called home. It made no sense. But, then, Dr. Berens had only a nodding acquaintance with Carmen Ellsworth.

Later, as Lillian walked toward the nurses' lounge for her coffee break, Dean Warner caught up with her in the corridor and revived the subject. "We're going to have a bit of a psychological problem before long," he warned. "Patty's gotten quite dependent on you, and she's a rather determined little kid. This business about not wanting to go home . . . she really means that."

Lillian stopped walking and the doctor stopped with her outside the lounge. "I know she means it. I've been trying to sell her on all the advantages of going home. The trouble is. . . ."

"There aren't many," Dr. Warner conceded. "Ordinarily, I'd have her signed out by the end of the week. With a good Special assigned to her at home, she'd do just as well recuperating there. Most children would do better." He scowled. "I just don't know. She won't even let me talk to her about it unless I promise you'll go with her. I think . . . Patty has it in her head that you're going to be a permanent fixture in her life."

"I've been trying to make her understand that I'm not," Lillian said. "So far, I haven't been too convincing, I'm afraid. She's latched onto that word 'special', and she simply refuses to believe that somebody 'special' can come and go the way maids and housekeepers have come and gone out of her life. Yesterday she got quite possessive and let me know I was *her* Special."

"That's not good. With everyone catering to them, sick kids get the idea that they can give orders."

"It wasn't a bossy sort of possessiveness, Doctor. She's just too young to understand that you can't keep. . . ." Lillian paused. "What I mean is, she wants to cling to everyone who loves her. . . ."

"And you do love her, of course."

Lillian's eyes met the doctor's for a stabbing instant. "We've been through a lot together," she said. "Patty's a very lovable child."

"You wouldn't consider. . . ."

"Going home with her? I don't think that would help, Doctor. Patty would only grow that much more dependent on me. Sooner or later, we'd have to make the break. I'd rather see her look to more permanent sources for affection."

"Yes, you're right."

"Besides, I wouldn't. . . ." Lillian caught herself in time. There was no point in revealing that Mr. Ellsworth was a factor in the decision; she was determined to close that door permanently.

"You wouldn't what?" Dean asked.

Lillian took time for a deep breath. "I wouldn't want to get any fonder of Patty myself," she said. "She'll feel differently when it's actually time to go home. Children are amazingly resilient." It was a hollow conclusion, and it seemed to Lillian that the doctor didn't accept it any more than she did, but the matter rested there until early that afternoon. It was then, shortly before Lillian was to go off duty, that Carmen Ellsworth came to pay an unexpected visit.

She was dressed in a high-fashion mini-dress that fit her as though Carmen had been dipped into the tangerine colored raw silk. Her coiffure, always elaborate, was even more so this afternoon; heads had turned as Patty's mother walked up the corridor, and she had

74

hesitated in the doorway to Room 406 the way a model pauses before stepping out on a fashion runway.

There was a cool exchange of greetings, and then Lillian invented an excuse to leave the room—Patty always required an excuse when her nurse wanted to leave her alone with her mother. When she returned to the room some twenty minutes later, Lillian found Mrs. Ellsworth's icy poise replaced by seething anger, and Patty in tears.

Lillian hurried to Patty's bedside. "Is something wrong, Honey?"

Carmen Ellsworth glared at her from her place at the foot of the bed. "You know perfectly well what's wrong," she hissed. "I've been paying you to take care of my little girl, not to alienate her affections."

The sharp accusation brought a fresh flood of tears from Patty, who reached out to grab Lillian's wrist. There was desperation in the almost painful clutch of her tiny fingers. Lillian was more aware of the child's need for serenity than she was of the hate-filled accusation that had been hurled at her. She was trembling, but she forced herself to sound calm. "I think you've misunderstood, Mrs. Ellsworth. Patty has enough love in her so that she can be fond of the staff here without. . . ."

"Don't patronize me, Miss Bryant!" The shrill voice had no place in a hospital room, and heaven knew it hadn't been cultivated in a charm school. "You know exactly what I'm talking about. Patty's just finished telling me she'd rather stay here with you than go home with me. Lovely! Is that what you were hired to do? Turn my own child against me?"

"Mrs. Ellsworth. . . ."

"It's the most despicable. . . ."

"Mrs. Ellsworth, whatever you have to say, for Patty's sake, I'd appreciate it if you waited until. . . ."

"I'm not going to be told what to say or when to say it. *Listen* to Patty! Ask her! She'll tell you just what you've taught her to say." Carmen Ellsworth's face was twisted with resentment and she seemed deaf to Patty's choking sobs. "Get her to repeat what she just said!"

Lillian used her free hand to massage Patty's shoulder—her other wrist remained firmly gripped. "It's all right, Patty," she murmured. "Your Mommy just misunderstood something. She loves you very much and she wants to be very, very sure you love her best of all. There's nothing to cry about, dear."

"You can spare me the maudlin speeches," Mrs. Ellsworth snapped. "I'm not so naive that I don't know what's going on behind my back." No mother who cared about her child's pain or confusion could have used that child so callously. Her ego had been injured, and she demanded Patty's help in proving her point. Bitter, using a cruel sarcasm that would have withered a strong adult, she demanded, "Go ahead, Patricia! Tell nursie what you just said to your own mother. Tell her you'd rather stay with *her* than. . . ."

Patty's cry, more terrible than any she had uttered during her most trying physical ordeals, was like a knife in Lillian's heart. Gently but firmly, she detached the little girl's fingers from her wrist. She whispered, "It's all going to be fine, Patty." Then she walked to the foot of the bed, fixed Carmen Ellsworth with a scathing gaze, and in a deadly tone that she hoped Patty would not hear, said, "Mrs. Ellsworth, you're upsetting my patient. I'm not going to add to her misery by telling you what I think of you, but I'm in charge here, and I'll give you exactly ten seconds to get out of this room." She barely sounded the rest of her ultimatum. "You can do whatever you like afterward, but if you aren't out of here in ten seconds, I'll use a technique I learned for subduing disturbed mental patients and I'll remove you by force."

Carmen Ellsworth's fury was unabated, but evidently the threatening monotone had frightened her. Her face blanched. Lillian watched the exquisitely painted mouth quiver, start to form a word, then quiver again. If ever the expression "speechless with fury" applied, this was the time.

I've gone as far as any nurse has the right to go, Lillian thought. Maybe further. This is my patient's mother I've ordered out of the room. I've threatened to eject her physically. If she insists upon staying, I'll have to keep my word. Either way, I'm finished here. And this isn't just another case. This is Patty, who needed me when almost everyone else thought she was dying. Patty, who needs my love the way she once needed my faith, my devotion as a nurse. Whatever happens, I'm going to be dismissed.

Tears threatened to well up in Lillian's eyes, infuriating tears. Carmen Ellsworth would interpret them as a sign of weakness, and the harangue would continue torturing Patty. The child was on the verge of hysteria now. Lillian clamped her lips tight and took a determined step forward.

Carmen Ellsworth let out a sound that was partially an expression of contempt but more a gasp of fear. In the next instant she was fleeing the room. No goodby kiss for her daughter, no assurance that she would return. Not until the woman had cleared the door did Lillian hear her venomous pronouncement: "You're going to regret this! I'll see to it that you're fired, you intolerable little snip!"

Mrs. Ellsworth's heels were heard clicking down the corridor, going so fast that she could not have heard Patty's heartbroken cry: *"Go 'way! I don't want you! I wanna . . . I wanna stay with my . . . my Lil'yun . . . I . . . hate . . . hate you-ou!"*

77

Lillian rushed to take the child into her arms. She was still comforting her when the relief nurse appeared at three o'clock. Just then Dean Warner came into the room to ask if he could have a word with her outside.

CHAPTER TWELVE

They had been sitting in one of the tiny consulting offices near the third-floor charge desk when a nurse interrupted the depressing conversation. Dean Warner had gotten up to respond to the knock on the door.

"Excuse me," the nurse said. She looked past the doctor, addressing her words to Lillian. "I was afraid you'd gone home, but Mrs. Tompkins said you hadn't checked out yet. Mr. Jessup left a message for you at the desk, Miss Bryant. You're to stop in at the administration office before you leave. Okay?"

Lillian thanked her and the nurse closed the door behind herself.

"Administration," Lillian sighed. "Does that mean I'm not just being taken off the case?—I'm getting thrown out of the hospital?"

Dean Warner resumed his seat at the desk. "Now you're being unreasonable, Lillian. I don't know what Mr. Jessup wants, but, believe me, it has nothing to do with what we've been discussing. I haven't said a word to him about what happened in Patty's room and I don't intend to. This is one of those . . . delicate things I wish I could avoid. Nevertheless, we can't have a repetition."

"I agree with you," Lillian said. "In fact, I'd give anything if I could undo the damage. Nobody has the right to make a child that miserable." Tears came close to engulfing her again—and Lillian squelched them with an outburst of pure anger. "I'm not going to say I'm

79

sorry, Doctor. If I had it to do over again, I'd do exactly what I did. My job is to. . . ."

"To protect your patient," the doctor placated. "You were absolutely within your rights. I've been trying to tell you, none of what I've been saying is to be construed as criticism."

"She had Patty in tears—half hysterical, and she didn't *care!* She kept tormenting the poor kid. Wanting Patty to back up her nasty accusation. Just . . . tearing that little girl apart emotionally. What makes a person like that tick? She's . . . she's absolutely heartless!"

Dean was silent for a few seconds, and he appeared embarrassed. After a while he said, "I'm not disagreeing with you, Lillian. Mrs. Ellsworth is. . . ." He shrugged. "Let's say she isn't geared emotionally the way . . . you . . . some of us are. At the same time, we can't forget that she's undergone quite a shock. She's undoubtedly feeling guilty about what happened to Patty. Her husband has been in the same boat, and I suspect they've relieved their guilt by accusing each other of negligence. That leaves us with a highly sensitive character to deal with, wouldn't you agree?"

"I don't think Mrs. Ellsworth has suffered any damage except to her ego," Lillian said. "I could tell her how to win Patty's love. But then she'd have to do it the way I did, by giving Patty the love she needs. Not by undermining someone else. Because I didn't *do* that, Dr. Warner! If anything, I've tried to convince her that . . . that her mother. . . ."

Lillian had lost the fight against tears. She felt them roll across her cheeks, too miserable to care what anyone thought. If Dean Warner wanted to chalk her up as a blubbering fool, that was his privilege; at least her conscience was clear.

"I know," he was saying. "I understand perfectly." He was using the pacifying, paternal tone that doctors use when they deal with emotional situations, soothing the troubled waters by speaking with exaggerated patience. He was treating Lillian like a spoiled child, leaning forward to touch her hand and repeating, "Please don't think I don't understand."

Lillian withdrew her hand in a furious jerking motion. "I'm a grown-up woman, Doctor. I'm not a three-year-old having a tantrum."

"I know that, too," he continued in that same soothing tone. "That's why I know you'll understand why we're going to have to make a change. Right or wrong, Mrs. Ellsworth *is* Patty's mother. If she's resentful, if she's jealous, it doesn't matter whether or not her attitude is justified. She's Patty's mother and you. . . ."

"I'm just part of the hired help," Lillian said bitterly.

"Those were *your* words, not mine. I know that a nurse can form an emotional attachment with a patient, especially when the patient is a child, and even more so when she's seen that child through a critical situation." Dean Warner got up from the desk and started to pace the small cubicle. "It's inevitable. Anyone who works in a hospital recognizes this. Certainly I do."

Lillian stared at the floor, regretting her outburst and struggling to get herself under control. "That's . . . in Patty's case, that's the understatement of the year, Doctor." Lillian got to her feet. "I hope you'll forgive me if I'm . . . half as fond of her as you are. If you don't mind, I'd appreciate not having to come in tomorrow. I'm sure a replacement shouldn't be hard to find . . . now."

He was at the door, barring her way. "You can't leave this suddenly. I don't care what her mother says, you've got to give Patty a chance to adjust."

"It's going to be twice as painful for her—and, just incidentally, for me, if we drag it out. I've listened to Patty cry her heart out for the last time, Doctor. I'm not going to put her through a miserable farewell scene, and I'm not going to be responsible for what happens if Mrs. Ellsworth comes at me again with . . . with more of her sickening swill!"

"Please!" Dean Warner's hand closed over Lillian's shoulders. "Lillian, please! I know you've been hurt, but I promise you . . . Carmen won't come around again while you're on duty. I'll see that she doesn't upset Patty again."

"You already told me it's best if. . . ."

"If you ease off the case, yes. Sure. You told me this morning that you didn't want to work at the Ellsworths' home. You know it isn't a healthy situation. . . ." Lillian bit her lower lip, nodding her agreement, letting the tears streak across her face. "All right, then. Stay until I'm ready to release your little gal. We'll both try to make it as easy as possible for her. Right?"

"I've always tried to do that," was Lillian's answer.

"I know you have. All I wanted to talk to you about . . . the reason I asked you in here was . . . it's not going to help Patty if we create a jealousy situation with her mother. Carmen . . . Mrs. Ellsworth has a lot to learn. It's going to be better for Patty, better all the way around, if we . . . if you do your job and try to stay as uninvolved emotionally as possible. Will you promise me that?"

Lillian searched for a reply, but found none.

"I know Patty isn't just . . . some flesh and bones to you . . . just a case with a chart and number. I *do* know that. All I want you to understand is that . . . you're going to go on to another case when she leaves. And another and another. But she's the only child Carmen has. With the two of them it's a lifetime proposition. I'd like to make it as pleasant for Patty as it can possibly be. I'm asking you to report back tomorrow morning and forget what happened today. Will you do that for me? Please?"

Lillian closed her eyes, nodding her head slightly.

"I knew you wouldn't let me down." Unbelievably,

someone had kissed her forehead—a gentle, brotherly kiss. For a moment, Lillian felt a surge of emotion she had long tried to suppress. *Was Dean going to take her into his arms? Had this conversation been only an excuse to be near her, to lead into a subject closer to his heart?*

"I've learned how completely I can depend on you," he was saying. And it was a doctor's voice again, the appreciative M.D. patting the loyal nurse on the head to express his thanks before she was dismissed. He had used his persuasive personality to rid himself of a troublesome problem. The nurse had been pecked on the forehead and pacified; there was nothing more to it than that.

"May I . . . go now?" Lillian choked on the words.

"Of course. I'm sorry I kept you this long." Lightly, using his professional cheer-up tone now, Dr. Warner added, "You've earned your rest tonight." He stepped aside and opened the door for Lillian. "When this case is finished, you'll have a good vacation coming to you."

Lillian didn't answer. She muttered a quick good-night and raced out into the corridor, determined not to cry in Dean Warner's presence again.

It was not until she had sobbed herself dry in a dark recess of the lounge washroom that she remembered the message from Vernon Jessup and started repairing her tear-swollen face in preparation for the puzzling summons from Administration.

CHAPTER THIRTEEN

Before she made her way to the Administration offices on Tri-City's main floor, Lillian stopped in the public phone booth next to the coffee shop and dialed her home number. Her call was answered on the second ring by a breathless, "Hello?"

"Bertha? I'm awfully sorry if I held you up. I got delayed . . . big mess involving Mrs. Ellsworth . . . I'll tell you about it later. I hope you didn't wait in the parking lot too long."

"The head nurse told me you were cooped up with Dr. Warner," Bertha said. She sounded disappointed; chances were that she had been expecting a call from Vernon Jessup. "I didn't wait around. Walked right over to the bus stop."

"Oh, that's good. There just wasn't any way to let you know, and it just occurred to me you were in a hurry to get home."

"I wasn't in any hurry." Bertha's gloomy tone was a distinct change from her early morning mood. "Vernon talked to me at lunchtime and said he wouldn't be able to make it tonight. Some kind of emergency board meeting, or something."

"That's a shame. Ah, well. Leave the steaks in the freezer and hang on. I imagine he took a rain check?"

"No. No, he was pretty vague about getting together another night." Bertha's attempt to sound flippant was unsuccessful. "No big deal. I had a rough day and I'd just as soon sit around in my old bathrobe and watch

84

the idiot box. I wasn't feeling up to getting all decked out and waiting on His Lordship tonight, so it's just as well."

"You'll make it up another night," Lillian assured her. "I know what you mean about a rough day. This one was the living end."

"I hear you had good news from the orthopedic man."

"We did. Yes, it's great news. Look, I'll tell you all about it when I get home."

"Are you still at the hospital? I defrosted those steaks . . . no point in wasting them. I'll get dinner going if you're coming straight home."

For no reason that she could understand, Lillian said, "I'm . . . not sure how soon I'll be able to get away Bertha. This stupid hangup is still going on here." Some uneasy instinct told her not to mention the call from Vernon Jessup's office. "Don't fix dinner for me. I'll grab something in the cafeteria here before I leave."

"What's going on over there?" Bertha demanded. "Sounds like some kind of inquisition."

"I'll tell you later," Lillian repeated. "I've got to run now."

A disquieting sense came over her when she finally dropped the receiver. Bertha had tried to sound indifferent, but her disappointment would have been obvious to a less perceptive listener. Too wrung out by her own emotional problems to have offered more encouragement, Lillian crossed the main floor lobby and stepped into the anteroom outside Vernon Jessup's office.

She had been sitting on the edge of her chair, across from the administrator's desk, for what seemed an interminable time, exchanging inanities with Vernon Jessup and wondering why he had called her in to see him. One thing was certain; Dean Warner had been right. The ponderous, slow-talking man behind the desk neither knew nor was concerned about Lillian's run-in with Carmen Ellsworth. On the contrary, he had been speaking in glowing terms about Lillian's service in Room 406. Finally, more nervous than curious, Lillian asked why she had been summoned.

Vernon Jessup's fingers drummed on his desk top and he seemed to be avoiding Lillian's questioning gaze. "The . . . matter I have to discuss," he said in his colorless tone, "doesn't . . . well, shall we say, doesn't lend itself to . . . this atmosphere."

Lillian frowned.

"What I . . . wanted to talk about is a . . . I suppose we might call it a . . . highly personal matter, and I was wondering if . . . Miss Bryant . . . Lillian . . . could you possibly arrange to have dinner with me this evening?" After stammering and turning a variety of blush-pink shades, Vernon blurted out his question with the abruptness of a sneeze. It was a performance worthy of a country bumpkin and totally absurd coming from an important executive. If the man had not appeared so painfully ill at ease, Lillian would have been amused.

"You're sure we can't talk about it here?" she asked. It seemed logical that Vernon was stewing about his relationship with Bertha. As shy and conservative as he was, it was even possible that he was on the verge of proposing to Lillian's friend and wanted some assurance that he would be accepted before taking the plunge. Lillian decided not to mention the "emergency board meeting" that he had used as an excuse to cancel his date with Bertha.

Feeling sorry for the paunchy bachelor, Lillian accepted his word that the matter of great importance he had to discuss could only be tackled over a serene dinner table. She agreed, also, that it might be best to meet somewhere other than the apartment. Until Bertha knew that the meeting involved her future, it might be awkward to explain.

Lillian found herself with nearly three hours to kill. For a while she was tempted to spend the time with Patty, making certain that her little patient was no longer disturbed by the incident with her mother. Then, remembering that Howard Ellsworth usually visited the child during the late afternoon, she changed her mind. And going home was unthinkable. She finally settled on the nurses' lounge, leafing through several magazines without interest, watching the early news on television, and finally making an effort to make herself presentable enough for the clandestine dinner date.

Lillian sat across from Vernon Jessup at one of the quiet dining rooms that attracted retirees who had come to while away their declining years in the Arizona sunshine. If Vernon wanted a serene atmosphere, he had selected the right place; the restaurant, dimly lighted and heavily carpeted, had all the excitement of a well-ordered funeral parlor.

There was awkward small talk while they ate their palatable but uninspired dinners, and it occurred to Lillian that the food, the decor and the conversation were admirably suited to her host's personality—respectable, proper, and uniformly dull. Yet Vernon's nervousness added an element of suspense to the occasion. It would have been rude to ask him to get to the point, but, as they finished dessert and dawdled over the coffee, Lillian had a barely controllable urge to ask why she had been invited here. Certainly not to hear a dissertation on the financing of a proposed neurological wing at Tri-City!

When Vernon Jessup finally broke the ice, he did so with as much care as if he had, indeed, been presenting a plan to the hospital board. For a few minutes,

Lillian listened to the man with stunned wonderment, thinking, my stars, he's giving me a report on his assets as a husband! I'm not Bertha's mother, she wanted to tell him. I don't really care how much money you have in the bank and in government bonds. It doesn't matter one fig that you have a splendid contract with Tri-City Hospital, that you don't have any bad habits, that you can afford to buy a lovely home in the suburbs, or that you have no dependent relatives!

He went on and on, as though he were filling in an application blank for an important position, and Lillian was just about to tell him that her approval was not necessary if he wanted to marry Bertha Risdon, when Vernon, who was not a man from whom you expected surprises, threw out the most shocking surprise imaginable: "As you know, Lillian, I'm not a rash person. I give a great deal of thought to any decision I make, whether it be a business decision or a . . . more personal one. You may have noticed that . . ." (there was a meaningful clearing of his throat) . . . "I have gone out of my way to spend time in your presence. You may have gathered from this that I . . . enjoy your company . . . and . . . as an admirer of feminine grace and beauty. . . ."

Lillian could only stare at him, dumbfounded, knowing what he was going to say next, yet not really able to believe what she was hearing.

"I have never been a believer in anything as illogical as love at first sight, but I must say that I was enormously attracted to you from that very first day when you came into my office to apply for your job at Tri-City. You really are . . . exceptionally beautiful, Lillian . . . and amazingly unworldly—a rare combination of qualifications that I have found irresistable."

Had she heard him correctly? *"Unworldly"!* The word was as anachronistic as Vernon himself; Lillian felt as though she might have been listening to some proper swain straight out of the Victorian age.

"Consequently," Vernon went on in his cut-and-dried manner, "after weighing the fact that you seem to be unattached, I've taken the liberty of asking you to . . . well, to consider . . . a permanent association. I'm confident that you would find such an arrangement pleasantly comfortable. I might add that I'm not the sort of person who looks upon marriage lightly. You'll find me a stable, completely dependable husband, and a devoted admirer."

It was inconceivable, but it had happened! Vernon Jessup, without so much as reaching out to take her hand, had just proposed marriage! Furthermore, he had said all he was going to say and was now looking at Lillian with an expectant expression, as though, having presented his case clearly and in detail, he had only to wait for her answer.

"I don't . . . really know what to say," Lillian told him. There was no doubting the man's sincerity—but it seemed so absurd! And, remembering Bertha's excited plans for this evening, so grossly unjust! "It just never occurred to me that. . . ." (How did you let someone like this down gently? How could you bring up the fact that another woman *did* love him, and that you looked upon him as a totally uninteresting relic from the past?)

Vernon came to her rescue gallantly. "Yes, I suppose you will want some time to think the matter over. I respect caution in people. Too many people, these days, leap before they look. Certainly. Mull it over in your mind, Lillian. I've given you all the facts concerning my age, you know the state of my health, my financial. . . ."

"Vernon, those things have nothing to do with choosing a husband or a wife!" The sentence had escaped Lillian, but she saw no reason for not expressing herself completely. "If I were in love with you, I wouldn't care if you were diabetic, penniless, or saddled with a whole flock of indigent relatives. Don't you see—when two people are in love, they don't know or care about anything else. Getting married isn't like applying for a job. It's . . . there's got to be. . . ."

"Too many people underrate the practical issues," Vernon pronounced solemnly. "Accounts for our deplorable divorce rate . . . these impetuous, thoughtless marriages, all storybook romance and absolutely no common sense."

"I know, but. . . ."

"Oh, don't suppose that I'm so stodgy that I overlook the more frivolous aspects. I've already told you that I find you extremely attractive physically. You're one of the prettiest, most personable young ladies, I have ever. . . ."

"I'm sorry," Lillian told him. (She wished the floor would open up and swallow her. *Bertha. What about Bertha!*) "I've . . . always respected you, Vernon, . . . I like you. As a friend, I . . . like you a great deal. But I've always assumed that you and Bertha. . . ."

"Bertha and I are just exactly that, and no more," Vernon said with a dismissing wave of his hand. "Good friends. I'm sure she's told you that I have never. . . ." His face colored, and Vernon seemed to be searching for a genteel way to explain what he meant. "I have always stayed within the bounds of propriety," was the way he finally expressed it; a cliché straight out of a turn-of-the-century manual for young lovers! He sounded smugly defensive as he added, "My friendship with Miss Risdon is purely platonic, I assure you. A fine woman, though not exactly suited to my aesthetic tastes. Now, a girl as pretty as *you* are, Lillian. . . ."

Somehow, she at last brought the ridiculous conversation to an end. Still, it wasn't completely over; in trying to be considerate, Lillian had not closed the door firmly enough. When Vernon dropped her off at her car in the personnel parking lot at Tri-City, he had not actually been told that marrying him was the farthest thing from her mind. He remained "within the bounds of propriety," fortunately, but he parted from Lillian in a cheerful frame of mind, convinced merely that she, like himself, did not plunge into serious arrangements without due consideration. He was convinced that when Lillian thought over the plan he had outlined she would see its advantages.

Sick at heart over her own weakness, and still bewildered by the incongruous proposal, Lillian headed homeward, dreading the confrontation with Bertha and hoping that she would be skillful enough to lie plausibly about how she had spent the evening. Above all, having experienced enough misery of her own for one day, she was determined to spare her the truth about her prospects for marriage with the man who appeared to Bertha to be "just about ready to propose."

CHAPTER FOURTEEN

During the weeks that followed, Lillian found herself in the position of a criminal who has committed no crime and yet falls into the trap of avoiding people, of inventing lies, and of seeing no happy ending to this miserable plight.

By day, there were confrontations with the Ellsworths to be avoided—though this was a lesser problem. Dean Warner had kept his word, and Carmen did not return for a visit to Patty's room during the early shift. According to the hospital "grapevine," Howard Ellsworth had moved to a hotel, was separated from his wife, and no longer visited his daughter. If Patty noticed her father's absence, she was unconcerned; at any rate, he was never mentioned.

Avoiding Vernon Jessup, however, was another matter. He not only continued his irritating visits to Patty's room (though by now it was clear that he came to call on the nurse instead of the patient), but Lillian found herself running into him constantly—in the third-floor corridors, during lunch, in the coffee shop. If these encounters could be written off as coincidences, Vernon's messages could not. At least once a week, and sometimes more often, Lillian was called to the administrator's office on one flimsy pretext or another. Each time, Vernon managed to ask if she was giving "serious consideration" to his proposal. It seemed inconceivable to Lillian that a man could keep Tri-City operating smoothly and still apparently be so dense. Telling him she didn't love him seemed to have had no effect—Vernon was confident that time would take care of that minor deficiency, providing all other factors were favorable. Short of telling him he was an insufferably thick-headed bore, there seemed to be no way for Lillian to shake him.

Evenings were more difficult. Bertha's soaring hopes had turned from disappointment to anxiety, then bitterness. After several weeks had gone by without any contact from Vernon Jessup, the bitterness began to be laced with suspicion. Certainly she was becoming aware of Lillian's command appearances at the administration office, and these pointless meetings were difficult to explain. The tension only increased when Bertha stopped asking questions. Now she brooded silently. Short of breaking her heart with the truth, and perhaps losing her as a friend, there was nothing for Lillian to do but endure the taciturn coolness and hope that Vernon would one day forget that she existed.

As if to counterbalance the loss of warm friendliness at home, Lillian found her relationship with Patty Ellsworth gaining strength with every day that passed. Medically, Patty needed only minor attention; her injured arm and her ribs were healing beautifully, she was beginning to take supported steps, and she needed no coaxing at mealtimes. Best of all, the memory of her accident seemed to have been erased from her mind. Apart from the fact that she was still hospitalized, she was living an almost normal little girl's life.

But Lillian was always present. Not because Patty needed a Special nurse any longer; the floor nurses could have attended to her needs as easily. For that matter, most of the staff wondered why Patty had not been discharged several weeks earlier. Lillian was there, she gradually discovered, because Patty refused to be separated from her, and during the playtime hours in the sun of the hospital's patio, during games that the two of them had invented, during story periods and long, chattering conversations with the child, Lillian learned that such a dependency was a two-way street. She looked upon Patty now with a love that went far beyond her compassion as a nurse.

On those few occasions when she allowed herself to think about the future, Lillian wondered how she would fill the terrible vacuum that would exist when Patty was no longer in her care. It was as though there had always been a Patty, as though the childish prattle and the sudden, heart-warming hugs and kisses had always been a part of her life. Yet, inevitably, their close association would have to come to an end. It was a time to be dreaded, and when Patty would stop in the middle of some game they were playing, fixing Lillian with her serious blue eyes and say, "You won't go away, will you, Lilly? You're always gonna play with me, aren't you?" it was wrong to give the answer Patty wanted to hear, but it was painful, too, to know that their days together were numbered.

And there was another love that could only end, ultimately, in an intensified loneliness. Dean Warner had returned to his busy practice. He came to see Patty on morning rounds, and Patty revealed that he also usually came to visit her before bedtime, but Lillian's own contacts with the doctor were brief and impersonal. There were rumors that he was seeing more of Carmen Ellsworth now that she was separated from her husband. Perhaps this was only the imaginative conjecture of nurses who thrived on gossip, but to Lillian the possibility was real enough. Why wait around for complete heartbreak? With every association building up to some sort of unpleasant climax, why not leave now?

For several days Lillian had been weighing the question of whether it would be more painful for Patty to subject her to tearful farewells or to shatter her confidence by simply leaving and letting someone else tell her that her "special friend" would not be back. It was a difficult choice. She had decided to ask Dean Warner's advice, when, all at once, the decision was made for her. Returning from the supply closet one morning with fresh linens for Patty's bed, she stiffened at the sight of Carmen Ellsworth. Patty's mother was standing just outside the closed door to Room 406, several suitcases on the floor next to her. She was talking, in what seemed to be an agitated manner, to Dean Warner.

As Lillian drew nearer, the conversation was cut off abruptly. She said hello to Mrs. Ellsworth without receiving an answer, nodded at the doctor, and was reaching for the doorknob when Patty's mother said, "You may as well tell her to get Patty's clothes packed now, Dean. I have a luncheon date downtown, and I'd like to be able to get away as soon as possible."

Lillian's breath congealed in her lungs. She looked at the doctor for an explanation.

"Mrs. Ellsworth is here to take Patty home," he said. "I was hoping we could have more time to get Patty adjusted to. . . ."

"What sort of adjustment does she need?" Mrs. Ellsworth cut in. "Look, Dean, we've been hashing it over long enough. I'm getting the fall shows ready, I'm up to my ears in work, and I can't keep running over here every afternoon when you've admitted Patty could have gone home weeks ago."

"With proper home care . . ." he began.

"I told you I've hired a perfectly capable practical nurse," Mrs. Ellsowrth said, her tone imperious now. "I'm sure you'll come by to see that everything's in order." She paused, turning a heavy-lidded gaze directly at Dean Warner. "At any time. Choose your own visiting hours."

"That isn't the point, Carmen. Psychologically, I don't like the idea of bursting in on Patty and telling her. . . ."

"Miss Bryant has had plenty of time to prepare

Patty for the trying ordeal of going home with her mother." Carmen Ellsworth's scathing inflections were not lessened by the sugary smile she aimed at Lillian. "Will you get my daughter's things ready, please? Just her clothes. I'll have someone pick up her toys later. I think we can dispense with the goldfish."

"I hope you'll let her take those, Mrs. Ellsworth," Lillian said. She was determined not to show her emotions before this smugly superior woman, but her voice quavered. "Patty's very fond of. . . ."

"All right, we won't quibble," Mrs. Ellsworth snapped. "But please hurry. I've got to get Patty settled and then drive back downtown before twelve-thirty." She indicated the suitcases with a careless wave of her hand. "When you get rid of those sheets, come and get these empties—and tell Patty I'll be along in a minute."

Lillian murmured, "Yes, Mrs. Ellsworth," and turned the knob, her insides leaden. The last thing she heard was Dean Warner saying, "I wish you had at least phoned me first, Carmen. It's going to be rough. . . ."

It was worse than rough. Lillian didn't have to bring the suitcases into the room, nor did she have a chance to explain the situation gently to Patty. Perhaps the child had overheard the conversation outside the door, or perhaps it was her highly developed sixth sense for knowing something was wrong. Change was in the air, and Patty had been shaken by too many changes in her first few years on earth.

Patty was seated in her wheelchair when Lillian came in to set the linens on the edge of the bed. She had been feeding her goldfish. The small box of fish food was in one hand, while the other hand gripped the leg of a bedside table. Patty looked beyond Lillian's forced smile with an expression that should never have appeared in a little girl's eyes. There was indescribable hurt written there, but Lillian saw defiance, too. And something else that said, "I know I'm going to lose, because I've always lost, but I'm still going to fight."

Lillian approached her hesitantly, keeping her voice gentle and affectionate. "Honey, guess what? Your Mommy got so lonesome for you that . . ."

"I won't go!" Patty's shrill cry filled the room. *"I won't! I won't! You said you were gonna play with me all the time!"*

Patty's scream had brought her mother and Dr. Warner into the room.

"Darling, I'm going to come and see you every. . . ."

Lillian's assurance was cut off by a terrifying wail. *"You* don't like me, *either.* She won't *let* you come! You *know* it. You were only *fooling* me. . . . you said . . . you said. . . ."

Lillian's arms had gone around the child. "Patty, I *do* love you," she whispered. "Oh, Patty, you don't think. . . ."

"Get away! Get away!" The fish food pellets spilled to the ground as Patty tried to free herself from the embrace. She was sobbing hysterically now, her words incoherent, but she held on to the table leg with one hand, like a drowning person clinging to a rock.

"Carmen. . . ."

Dr. Warner's soft plea went unheeded. "I think we can do without a big scene, Patricia," Mrs. Ellsworth said. "Mommy has all kinds of lovely surprises waiting for you at home. A big, new dollhouse, and a wonderful lady who just adores little girls . . ."

Patty screamed, "No! You can't make me go!" But her sobs revealed that she knew better.

"Maybe if you let me talk to her for a while," Lillian said quietly. Patty's cries were tearing at her heart and her body had started an uncontrollable trembling. "I think I could. . . ."

"This is ridiculous!" Carmen Ellsworth brushed past Lillian and pried Patty's hand from its tenacious hold

97

on the table. "This is precisely what I've been complaining about, Dean. Allowing the child to be spoiled rotten, pumping her full of poison about me until she acts as though I'm an ogre." Her voice rose sharply. "That will do, young lady. There isn't a thing in the world wrong with you, and I'm not going to tolerate any more of this nonsense!"

Patty's defiant spirit had been broken, along with the grip of her hand. She was only crying now, gasping for air and making pathetic little sounds that had brought an orderly and one of the floor nurses to the open doorway.

"The least you can do. . . ." Dr. Warner started.

"The least *everyone* can do is stop catering to this child's tantrum!" Mrs. Ellsworth said angrily. "What Patty needs is a firm hand and a lot less indecisive quibbling." She wheeled Patty's chair forward and addressed her words to Lillian. "You'll help me immensely if you leave the room, Miss Bryant. And send one of the other angels of mercy in here to get these suitcases packed."

Lillian looked to Dean Warner, her eyes brimming, asking the question.

The doctor's face had taken on a sickly pallor, but he spoke evenly. "It might be best, Miss Bryant. We don't want to prolong. . . ." He stopped short of saying "the agony," but the words were implied in the way he was staring at Patty.

Lillian made a move toward the little girl, every fiber of her being urging her to close Patty in her arms and to comfort her. A chill look from Mrs. Ellsworth stopped her. *I'm not even going to kiss her goodbye,* she thought desperately. *I'm never going to see Patty again, and she thinks I've failed her. She'll never trust anyone, she'll never believe she's really loved. . . .*

"*If* you don't mind," Patty's mother said.

Lillian's own tears escaped her. She placed a hand over her mouth to muffle a sob and rushed toward the door, edging past the orderly and several nurses who had by now gathered there. This was part of Patty Ellsworth's "fan club," each of them torn by the child's pitiful sobbing, none of them in a position to express their inner wrath. This was the patient's mother taking her daughter home; what could they say?

She was hurrying down the corridor when Dean Warner caught up with her. He sounded stern as he stopped Lillian. "This isn't the kind of behavior I'd expect from a nurse, Miss Bryant. I would have preferred a less abrupt departure, but you know hysterics aren't going to make it easier for Patty. If you carried on this way every time one of your patients leaves the hospital. . . ."

Lillian whirled to face him. "Patty's not just another patient! Was she 'just another patient' when they brought her in here, Doctor? When you gave up the rest of your practice to sit up with her night after night?" The audience that had been listening to the scene in Room 406 had turned its attention to Lillian now, but she was beyond caring. "You asked me to believe she was going to live, remember, Doctor? You wanted me to pray for her . . . to help you keep her alive . . . to *love* her. And I do love her more than that—that plastic mannequin who calls herself a mother is ever going to love her!"

"Miss Bryant. . . ."

"Don't try to pacify me!" Lillian cried. "You know what she's doing to that poor kid! You know what she'll do to her!"

"Mrs. Ellsworth is. . . ."

"Please don't tell me again that she's the patient's next-of-kin and I'm just Patty's nurse." Lillian shook the tears from her wet face, more furious now than miserable. "It didn't have to be this painful for Patty. If that nasty witch had a heart . . . if you weren't so calloused that you think . . . you think I'm just a . . . just a medical machine. . . ."

"I'm very sorry," he was saying. "I've already told you I didn't plan it this way. There's simply nothing. . . ."

"You could have. . . ." Lillian choked on her words. She wasn't sure what Dean Warner could have done, but her frustration demanded a final, devastating outburst. "You're too calloused to understand! I don't know how I could have fallen in love with someone so. . . ."

She had said that aloud! Loud enough for everyone in the corridor to have heard. For a long, terrible moment, aware of Dean Warner's shocked stare, Lillian stood trembling with her still unspent rage. Then, as humiliation closed over her, she stifled another sob and ran. The nurses' lounge was ten million miles away. An eternity later, Lillian collapsed on one of the divans and let her tears run their course.

CHAPTER FIFTEEN

It was just noon when Lillian collected herself enough to move from the divan in the lounge. Splashing cold water on her face, with no more tears left inside her, she was only conscious of several depressing facts: Patty was gone. There would be a new case now —if her emotional scene had not disqualified her for another assignment. Nurses just didn't humiliate doctors publicly. They didn't race down hospital corridors crying like children or berating a patient's relatives.

Suppose she *was* finished at Tri-City, then? Did it matter? The situation with Vernon Jessup was intolerable. Bertha's moodiness had made their after-duty hours at home gloomy periods to be dreaded. And Dean Warner? He had used her services and dismissed her with a cold lecture about how nurses ought to behave. Besides, she had told him her secret; facing him again would mean complete humiliation.

Lillian looked at her puffy face in the washroom mirror and shuddered. The man she loved had looked at that face, tear-splotched, reddened, and distorted with anger . . . and then had gone back to the poised perfection of Carmen Ellsworth, sympathizing with her problem and perhaps even agreeing with Patty's mother that an overly solicitous R.N. was to blame for the child's unstable temperament. Mrs. Ellsworth had a rational outlook. If something had to be done, it should be done as quickly and efficiently as possible— and wasn't this the way a hospital functioned? She's not only beautiful, Lillian thought glumly, maybe she's better equipped to be a nurse than I am. She got Patty out of this hospital, didn't she? Maybe Dean admires her no-nonsense attitude. Maybe I had no business loving Patty so much I wanted to keep her here.

Dean Warner . . . Patty. The two loves whirled into a muddled, inseparable whole. Hopeless. Senseless. When should she leave? Lillian dried her face with a paper towel and firmed her decision. *Now.* Before she was lectured, fired, proposed to again, or scowled at by a brooding roommate. *Get out now.* She began the almost futile process of making her face look presentable again.

Stopping off at Administration was more a perverse action than a practical one. Lillian justified the visit to Vernon Jessup's office on the grounds that her next job application, wherever she went, would not be made easier if she didn't give formal notice that she was leaving Tri-City Hospital. Besides, she would have to leave a forwarding address for her last check. But once she stood in front of Vernon's desk she realized that she could have managed these two details by phone. There was still a residue of anger rankling inside her. It burst out seconds after Vernon Jessup had said, "You can't leave us this way, Lillian. Whatever's bothering you, I'm sure we can make it right."

"You can't make it right," Lillian told him curtly. "As a matter of fact, you're one of the reasons why I can't go on working here."

Vernon got to his feet, stunned. "My dear girl, if anyone has tried to make your job here pleasant . . . why, I'm not merely interested in you professionally, dear. You know that I. . . ."

"I know that you're a philandering old fool who's used a very dear friend of mine for a . . . a free meal ticket!" Vernon's indignant gasp had no effect on Lillian. "Bertha *loves* you. But she's too good for you. You don't deserve her, and you ought to consider

102

ourself lucky to have someone like her to tolerate
our . . . your old-fossil attitude."

"You can't possibly mean what you're saying, Lil-
ian. Something has upset you and. . . ."

"I mean *exactly* what I'm saying," Lillian insisted.
Mercifully, she was past the point of tears, and she
poke with a deadly incisiveness. "Proposing marriage
o me behind Bertha's back! What do you know about
ne? We don't have one single, solitary thing in common. About all you've talked about was a pretty face.
Well, it doesn't look very pretty now, and I don't care.
If you weren't so shallow, you'd have seen Bertha
as the really beautiful person she is. You'd look
inside. . . ."

Vernon was obviously miffed. He sounded like the
colorless business machine he was as he protested,
"This is intolerable, Lillian. I won't have you castigat-
ing me because I was incautious enough to admire
an attractive young lady. Now, if you're quite
finished. . . ."

"If you want to know something about beautiful
faces, ask Howard Ellsworth," Lillian concluded. "I'm
sure *he'd* tell you he married the ugliest woman in the
world!"

Senseless. What good did it do to make another dis-
turbance, to lose control of herself, spouting off all the
irritating thoughts that had been rankling inside her for
weeks? Lillian sighed. "You're right, Mr. Jessup.
Something else *did* upset me. And I'm . . . just getting
a lot of petty annoyances off my chest."

She thanked Vernon, after that, for his consideration in hiring her, and they made the polite, civilized
noises of saying goodbye and wishing each other good
luck in her future. Lillian was promised a letter of recommendation wherever she chose to work, and, somehow, she finally was out of the office and out in the
brilliant sunlight of the parking lot.

It wasn't until she was halfway home that she remembered she had left no address to which her check could be forwarded. It struck her then, with the impact of a fierce blow to her stomach, that she *couldn't* have left a new address. Because she didn't know where she was going.

CHAPTER SIXTEEN

Lillian had a vague remembrance of stopping at the bank to withdraw her small savings, and then of sitting in a park, trying to adjust her mind to the radical step she had just taken, and of rehearsing the words with which she would explain her sudden decision to Bertha: *Blame it on the situation with Dean Warner. Say nothing about Vernon Jessup. If nothing was said, maybe Vernon would come to his senses and Bertha would accept him back without resentment.*

It was nearly four o'clock, and she had gone without lunch. Feeling light-headed, but armed with a plausible explanation, Lillian opened the apartment door and stepped into the living room. She sensed instantly that something was wrong. Her luggage, topped with several shoe boxes and a bulky car coat that would not fit into a suitcase, sat near the door. Bertha was not in the room, nor was she in the kitchen, which was visible from the front door.

Lillian stopped to examine the neat pile of possessions surrounding her luggage. Everything was there. Everything she owned. Her heart began an erratic tattoo. What did it mean? Half hoping she wouldn't receive an answer, she called out Bertha's name.

Several seconds went by before Lillian heard a bedroom door opening down the hall. Hardly breathing, she stood motionless, listening as the familiar clomping steps approached. Then, suddenly, Bertha was in the hall doorway, still wearing her uniform, but looking rumpled and unkempt, as though she had been lying down in the overstarched white outfit. Her hair was disheveled, its fake platinum color clashing garishly with her lobster red face.

For another instant—during which Lillian thought, "Oh, no! Not more tears! I've had enough of crying to last me the rest of my life!"—there was a deadly silence. Then, her voice raspy, Bertha said, "I've packed everything for you. Now get out!"

Lillian gaped at her. "Bertha, what's wrong? I haven't. . . ."

"Don't tell me what you've done and what you haven't done. Just get out. I don't even want to look at you." Bertha's scorn could not have been more complete. *"My best friend!"*

Lillian moved toward her. "Bertha, I don't know what you've imagined or what kind of rumors you've been listening to, but I can explain what . . ."

"I don't want to hear anything you've got to say. You weren't satisfied chasing Howard Ellsworth, breaking up *one* home! You had to make a grandstand play for a man you don't even care about. Getting Vernon to fall all over himself for you, when you knew what he meant to. . . ." Bertha stopped to control her shaky voice. "You knew how much . . . he meant to me."

"I *do* know," Lillian pleaded. "And I care. Please believe me, Bertha, there's absolutely nothing between us."

"I suppose that's why you've been going out with him. Coming home and lying to me, telling me you'd gone to a movie. One of the aides saw you holding hands with him at The Candlelight House. Go on, deny it! Tell me you weren't there!"

"He asked me out to dinner once. I thought he wanted to talk to me about you. . . ." Bertha's disbelieving glare made the explanation sound like a lie, even to Lillian's ears. "It's true! I had no idea he. . . ."

"He *what?*" Bertha challenged.

"I didn't want to tell you this. But it was only because I didn't want you to be hurt. I knew he'd get over . . . his silly infatuation."

"I supposed he asked you to marry him! And you weren't interested. Oh, no. But you kept sneaking around to his office, encouraging him, probably laughing at me. Plain, stupid, ugly me!" Bertha raked her hands through her brightly bleached hair, leaving it looking like a nylon dishmop. "What a laugh *this* must have given you. Old Big Bertha, trying to make herself look beautiful! Going out and buying a slinky dress to . . . drape on her scarecrow figure."

"Oh, Bertha, please! I never thought anything of the kind!" Touched by her friend's misery, Lillian moved to put an arm around her. "I couldn't be fonder of you. You know I wanted. . . ."

Bertha moved away from the unwelcome contact with a savage jerk. "Leave me alone! You must be awfully proud of yourself. It's so easy for you, with your pretty face and. . . ."

"How easy *has* it been?" Lillian cried. "You've known for a long time that I'm in love with Dean Warner. A lot of good. . . ."

"Sure! And just because he bruised your little ego, you had to go out and prove you're irresistible to every man who crossed your path! At first, I didn't want to believe what I heard about you. Don't worry, people know what goes on! When you went out with Patty's father, I swallowed that sweet, innocent story of yours. I even called you *naive*. You—*naive!* That's the stupidest. . . ."

"Bertha, will you get hold of yourself and listen to me?"

"I've heard all I want to hear. Your bags are packed. Now just get out, and don't ever let me see you again!" Bertha turned on her heels and ran back into the hall, her sobs almost as painful to hear as Patty's had been.

Lillian hurried after her, the bedroom door slamming in her face, then hearing the lock being turned from inside the room. "Bertha, listen to me! You didn't have to throw me out. I only came back here to pack my things. I've quit my job."

There was no reply except the muffled sound of Bertha crying.

"I've already told Vernon I'm finished here. I told him what I thought of him . . . that he doesn't deserve you." Lillian jiggled the doorknob. "Let me talk to you, please! It's not like you think it is, Bertha, honestly."

Still no response. Lilllian made one more desperate attempt at reconciliation. "You'll find out that I haven't lied to you. I was leaving anyway. Let me tell you why, Bertha. Please?"

She might as well have addressed her arguments to a stone wall.

Earlier today, it would have seemed to Lillian that there was no way for her to feel more depressed. She knew better now. For a long while she waited outside the door, hoping that her message would sink in, that the tears would stop and Bertha would be ready to listen to reason. When it became obvious that the door had been closed finally and completely, Lillian returned to the living room and slowly, still without a destination, began carrying her luggage out to the car.

CHAPTER SEVENTEEN

Lillian had gotten as far as a downtown hotel in Phoenix—a plush spot that she normally would have considered beyond her means, except that in her confused state she had been afraid to drive further.

Somehow, emotional exhaustion had tired her body as well as her mind, and she slept. She awoke to a dark room and to hunger pangs, slowly orienting herself to where she was and why she was there, and then flicking on the light to discover that it was nearly midnight.

It seemed somewhat absurd to have her stomach growling when she had fled to this lonely cell out of heartbreak. Then she remembered that she had eaten nothing since her light breakfast at six-fifteen that morning. A shower would help to clear her fogged brain, then, hopefully, hot soup or a dinner, if the coffee shop she had noticed on the first floor was still serving. Certainly she couldn't stay here. *Get back to normal, decide where you're going, set the alarm for six and leave early. Los Angeles, maybe—Your original destination. There were plenty of hospitals there. Begin all over, get busy, work hard and forget.*

Except for a waitress, a porter who was sweeping the floor behind the counter, and one lone customer who sat in a corner booth with his face buried in the evening paper, the coffee shop was deserted. Lillian was immensely relieved; dining alone at this hour in a roomful of strangers would have added to her uneasiness. She selected the smallest table available near the door, and had given her selection from a breakfast menu to an indifferent waitress, when the newspaper on the opposite side of the room was lowered. It was an impossible coincidence, but the face that stared at her, first in surprised recognition and then with apparent pleasure, belonged to Howard Ellsworth.

He got up, tossing the newspaper aside and carrying his coffee cup to her table, looming over her, more expansive and more nattily suited than ever. Inanely, after Howard had greeted her and expressed his astonishment at seeing her here alone Lillian asked, "What are *you* doing here?"

He set his coffee cup down and made himself comfortable in the chair opposite Lillian's, grinning widely. "That's a fine question. This is home. I *live* here! Hasn't anyone told you?"

"I'd . . . heard you moved out of your apartment, but I didn't. . . ."

"Don't look embarrassed. It's no big secret. Carmen's filed for a divorce on grounds of mental cruelty and I'm not contesting. Nothing at all hush-hush about it. What about you?"

"I'm . . . on my way to . . . Los Angeles," Lillian stammered.

She felt her face coloring under Howard's questioning stare. "Oh, really? You didn't get very far."

"Well, I thought I'd rest up and get an early start in the morning."

"I see. Quit your job?"

"Yes, I . . . it was one of those impulsive things. I get tired of being in a rut, and then I just up and take off. I've done it before." Lillian feigned a careless little laugh. "You know. Carefree. I hate feeling tied down to one place. Same old faces, same old things to do and see."

Howard nodded sagely. "Yeah. I know." He took his time lighting a huge cigar, puffing on it and then studying the plume of smoke he had exhaled. "Finished with your case, I imagine. I phoned the hospital this afternoon. I had in mind dropping in to see Patty, but it occurred to me that she might be at home by now. Good hunch. Gal at the switchboard said the kid had been signed out before noon."

Lillian suspected that he hadn't believed her earlier story, but Howard seemed to accept the fact that she had left Tri-City when her patient had been released.

There was a brief silence while Howard stared at his cigar end and the waitress brought Lillian's coffee. Then he asked solemnly, "How was she?"

"Patty?"

"When you left her. Not all scarred up? Not crippled or. . . ."

"She's fine. I think Dr. Warner may order some cosmetic surgery later. When he sees how her shoulder scars shape up. Other than that. . . ." Lillian felt a surge of melancholy, remembering. "Patty's made phenomenal progress. She'll be walking before you know it. Except for a few scars, she'll forget she ever had an accident."

"She's lucky," Howard muttered.

"You aren't still torturing yourself . . . ?"

"No. No, I think you helped me through that guilt game, Lillian, thanks. I'm still sorry. I wish I could take that day back and do it over again, but . . . I know it won't help to agonize over something that wasn't intentional." Howard was somber for a few seconds and then ground the freshly lighted cigar out in an ash tray. "I'm not saying I wasn't all turned inside out emotionally after it happened. I probably owe you a big, fat apology, Lillian. Can you look at it this way? I was getting a steady diet of what a rat I was, and I was ripe for the first female who came along and reminded me that I'm still a human being. You just hap-

111

pened to be the unlucky victim. I wasn't too bad, was I?"

"Just what you said you were," Lillian assured him. "A human being. Very, very human."

"If I made any cockeyed promises . . . I know I had too much to drink that night we went out to dinner. . . ."

"You made no promises."

He seemed relieved. "I'm glad. What I need is this period I'm having right now. No entanglements. Working like hell. Lots of time alone to . . . sort of clear the cobwebs out of here." Howard tapped his skull with a thick forefinger. "After you make an enormous mistake, if you're wise, you shift into neutral and coast for awhile. Too many people get right back on the freeway and . . ." he chuckled at his prolonged analogy, ". . . get their gears stripped."

It was advice worth remembering. Lillian sipped at her coffee, then nodded her agreement.

Howard covered a yawn. "We-e-ll, they say something good comes out of the crummiest situations. For Patty's sake, now that I'm out of the picture, I hope Carmen and Dean will get back together again. He deserves a better break, understand, but Carmen's not getting any younger. It takes more time every day to get her looking the way she does. I imagine she's thought it out in that crafty little brain of hers and figured out she could do worse. Successful doctor. Time she gets fed up running that business of hers and wants to pamper herself a little more, her first husband might start rating a little higher in her book."

Lillian had been listening in stunned silence. Now she barely sounded the question: "Her first . . . *husband?*"

Howard looked surprised. "That's not news to you, is it? We tried to keep it quiet, but you know how word gets around. We figured, time Patty got a few years older, we'd have to either pull up stakes or tell

112

her the truth. I don't know how Carmen figured on keeping it a secret, living in the same town as the kid's father. Not that Dean was ever going to tell Patty. But —you know." Howard shrugged his massive shoulders. "If one person knows, sooner or later everybody knows. I sure thought you knew it by now . . . being around Dean and Carmen this long."

"I don't even . . . understand it now," Lillian said.

It was a simple story, as she now learned. Dean Warner had been in the last year of his residency at Tri-City when he had met the girl who was then named Carmen Fournier. They had known each other only a short time when they had gotten married, and in an even shorter time Carmen had decided that being the wife of a low-salaried resident doctor who spent most of his time on call at the hospital was not her dish of tea. She had run off to New York for two weeks—long enough to determine that she was a highly qualified fashion model, and then she had returned to Phoenix by way of Reno, Nevada. In a grand total of nine weeks, she had honeymooned, whetted her taste for a glamorous career, and freed herself of a husband who had confused infatuation with love.

"I could be wrong," Howard said. "Maybe it wasn't just Carmen's beautiful pan and that sexy shape. I'm probably judging Dean by what happened to me. I know that's all I saw. Maybe he was in love with her. For all I know, he still is."

"But Patty. . . ."

"Carmen didn't know there was going to *be* a Patty until she had her divorce papers in her pocket. What's more, she didn't let Dean know until *after* the kid was born. I think she came back here as soon as she found out she was going to have a baby. I'm not sure. That gives you an idea how much conversation I've had with my wife. How well I knew her before I got hooked."

Lillian's ham and eggs arrived, but although she had been famished a few minutes earlier, she was barely able to swallow her food. (Howard had predicted that Dean and Carmen might "get together again". No one who loved Patty could fail to wish that it were so. You had to get busy. Coast along, avoid entanglements, work hard and . . . what was it Howard had said? Clear away the cobwebs?)

"Well, the upshot was that I came into the picture before the kid was born, believe it or not," Howard went on. "Dean was struggling along with a brand new practice, just about keeping his head above water. Carmen's never said so, but I think he tried to get back together with her when he learned about the baby coming. I know he was paying all of Carmen's expenses when I met her. She moved into an apartment building I'd just finished putting up, and I remember she complained that her ex-husband was a cheapskate. I had him pegged as a real heel; rich doctor making his poor pregnant wife worry about scraping up the rent.

"I felt sorry for Carmen, and I started hanging around. I didn't know, then, that Dean was probably living on beans, trying to keep Tootsiebelle in one of the most expensive pads in town. All I knew was that I was the big hero. I sure as heck could provide for this gorgeous, helpless little doll. And I did. You better believe it, girl. I sure did. What's more, I married her two weeks after Patty was born."

"And Dr. Warner let you. . . ."

"Adopt the kid? Yeah. He stewed about it for awhile. I didn't know at the time how hard he was taking it. You know, he's crazy about that girl."

Lillian recalled the day when she had been called in on Patty Ellsworth's case, remembered "Docky Dean's" almost insane efforts to save the child's life. "I know," she said. "Yes, I know that much."

"We had a few sticky meetings. I was still seeing myself as a gallant knight in shining armor and Warner as a full-blown villain. Carmen helped me along there. Fact is, the doc and I have never been what you'd call "buddy-buddy." What I didn't know was that it probably tore the guy's gut to give Patty up.

"When Carmen let him know that she was going to stay right here in Phoenix, Dean thought about going somewhere else," continued Howard. "And then we worked it out so that he could get to see the kid whenever he wanted to. As her doctor. It was Dean's idea not to let Patty know he was her father. I guess he figured she'd be better off having a stable family life. Mama, Papa, baby-girl. He was thinking about Patty when he made that decision. At the time, Carmen had me convinced he was. . . ." Howard pulled a fresh cigar out of his inside coat pocket. ". . . Never mind what."

"You know better now?" Lillian ventured.

"*Do* I! You know how old Patty was when my wife started this big venture of hers? Six weeks! Six weeks old. On her second honeymoon, yet! All the money and clothes a woman could possibly want. Her own sports car. Everything you can get with money. *She* had to get herself involved in a modelling agency. T.V. shows. Fashion shows. Dinner dates with merchandise managers. *Anything* but staying home and taking care of that baby." The second cigar was lighted with unsteady hands. "Look, I'm not at home around kids. Never had one of my own, don't know what to say to them, don't know how to take care of them. I don't have to tell you that. The one thing I *did* know was that Carmen neglecting me wasn't one tenth as bad as dumping that baby on one dumb maid after another. I never was much of a father to Patty, but at least I knew that."

Lillian had managed to rearrange the food on her plate, choke down a piece of toast, and swallow her coffee. She felt tired, suddenly. Sick of the whole story and her own miserable involvement in it. Howard must

115

have noticed her fatigue. "I guess you'll be wanting to hit the sack. Leaving for L.A. early in the morning and all."

"Yes."

He reached across the table to pump her arm with a clumsy handshake. "Well, all the luck in the world, Honey. Hope you have a ball in California. I s'pose you're all excited about the big change? Can't wait to get out there and tackle the big city?"

"Oh, yes. Yes, I'm terribly. . . ."

"Did I say something wrong? Lillian?"

He was all concern, and Lillian was making a thorough-going fool of herself, crying again for no reason at all. No reason, except that a little girl she had learned to love might . . just *might* see her mother and father reunited. And wouldn't anyone have wished that for Patty? As dearly as Patty loved Dean Warner, wasn't that what *everyone* wanted for her?

"I don't know what I said." Howard Ellsworth was helping Lillian out of her chair, a huge mass of confusion and apology. "I have a talent for saying the wrong thing. You don't really want to go away. Is that it? Somebody give you a hard time? Some creep at Tri-City? I've got some pull in this town. You say the word, Lillian, and I'll pin their ears back. Was it Jessup? Anybody I know? Somebody hurt you, kiddo? Anybody I know?"

Lillian drew a deep breath of air into her lungs and pulled herself together. "It wasn't anyone you know," she lied.

"Okay. Okay, it's not my business. Go on back to your room and sleep it off. Let me get the check."

She realized, later, when she had reached the sanctity of her room, that she had neither thanked Howard Ellsworth nor said goodbye to him. He hadn't deserved to have her run off that way without an explanation. For all she knew, he was blaming himself for her blubbering departure, adding her to his list of unjustified guilts.

Still later, as the first fingers of dawn pierced Lillian's room after a sleepless night, she remembered something else: the look on Howard's rugged face when she had said, "It wasn't anyone you know." He was tough and crude in an honest sort of way, and he hadn't been extremely perceptive in choosing a mate for life. But Howard Ellsworth's sensitivity had been sharpened by a series of bad experiences, and he knew a lie when he heard one. He had been sympathetic. And he hadn't believed her.

CHAPTER EIGHTEEN

Lillian reached to shut off her alarm clock and then discovered that the ringing that had awakened her hadn't come from the clock at all. Still groggy, having dozed off just at dawn, she lifted the telephone from its cradle. It had to be Howard Ellsworth. No one else knew she was here.

Her cracked, "Hello?" brought a response from a familiar voice.

"Lillian? Is that you, Lillian?" The voice sounded troubled. "You know who this is?"

"Bertha? What's . . . ?"

"Honey, I don't want to go into a long thing about how sorry I am and how stupid I was. Vernon called me last night. He's a nut, you know it? But at least he knows he's a nut and he's *my* nut, so I don't want to talk about that. Lil. . . ."

"You mean he. . . ."

"Never mind about us. He came over later and told me . . . listen, I didn't even have to wear the pink dress. It's all fine and I was wrong, so will you let it go at that? He wants to marry me, that's how crazy everything is. And he wouldn't have ever asked me if you hadn't. . . ." Bertha sucked in a huge swallow of air that came across the phone wires like the sound of a typhoon. "Look, that's not why I'm calling. We can both tell you how sorry we are later. Mr. Ellsworth called here last night, too. Got me out of bed in the middle of the night—darn near gave me a heart attack."

"He called *you* . . . ?"

"Yeah, yeah, he said he'd seen you and you were acting funny-peculiar and he was worried something was wrong. So he got your home number from the hospital and . . . Lillian? Listen, I know you'll want to get over to the hospital. Don't give me any hogwash about how you don't want to get involved again—this is serious."

Lillian's muscles tightened. "What is it?"

"Your little girl is back. Dr. Warner's been driving me out of my skull trying to get in touch with you. I knew where you were, but I didn't know if you wanted *him* to know, so . . . listen, don't you know enough to answer your phone? I've been ringing for. . . ."

"What's the matter with Patty?" Lillian demanded. Suddenly, nothing else was important. "Did he say?"

"He didn't say anything except that she's back at the hospital and he needs you there. So don't kill yourself getting over there, but don't waste any time, either. Okay?"

"I'll leave right away," Lillian promised. She started to drop the phone back into its receiver.

"And Lillian . . . ?"

"Yes?"

"Lillian, I want you to know. . . ."

"Hey, I'll talk to you later. . . ."

"I just want you to know . . . Vernon and I . . . after last night . . . you wouldn't believe me, but. . . ."

"You're very happy?" Lillian asked impatiently.

"We're *very* happy. I'll see you at the hospital. Hurry on down."

Lillian hurried. An alert traffic policeman, had he been anywhere along the route between downtown Phoenix and Tri-City Hospital, could have written a

119

mile-long string of tickets that morning to one lone female driver.

There was nothing to be learned at the third-floor charge desk except that Patty Ellsworth had been readmitted in the early hours of that morning, that her condition was undetermined as yet, and that Dr. Warner was in the room with his patient.

"Dr. Warner sent for me," Lillian said. "Is it all right if I go into . . . ?"

Lillian's former head nurse eyed her hesitantly. She had been notified that Miss Bryant no longer worked at Tri-City. "I'd suggest you wait for Dr. Warner in the reception room," the head nurse said. She might have been addressing a stranger, and Lillian felt, suddenly, like an outcast.

All the faces she saw passing the nurses' station were familiar. If she had been in uniform, this might have been just another routine day. Except that on ordinary days staff people who met her in the corridor smiled and asked, "How's our little gal doing this morning?" Now Lillian was asking the question, and so far there had been no satisfactory answer. Disconsolate, she made her way back to the small waiting room near the elevator cages.

Lillian had been sitting on one of the plastic settees for perhaps ten minutes—though the clock seemed to be dragging its hands—when one of the elevators disgorged Carmen Ellsworth.

The woman was incredible, Lillian thought. At an hour when most women are having difficulty keeping their eyes open, Patty's mother looked as though she were ready to pose for a *Vogue* photographer. She was wearing a smartly tailored suit of some nobby, melon-green fabric. Not one hair on her head was out of place. Her makeup was flawless, and only when the bright morning sunlight from a high window at the end

120

of the waiting room struck her face were the tiny age lines around her eyes visible.

Incredible, too, was Carmen Ellsworth's attitude. She flashed her theatrical smile at Lillian, behaving as though they had always enjoyed the warmest personal regards for each other. "Hello, dear!" she said. *Unbelievable!* The greeting sounded wholly sincere. Maybe she doesn't *have* any real emotions, Lillian guessed. Maybe even her anger and resentment aren't any more genuine than her loves!

"I dashed downstairs for coffee," Carmen said. She walked across the narrow floor space to sink gracefully onto the same settee Lillian was occupying, fishing in a mammoth petit-point handbag for a cigarette case and an engraved gold lighter that matched it. "Did you just get here? I must have missed you on the elevators."

"Dr. Warner called for me," Lillian said. She straightened her posture, challenged by the other woman's perfect poise. "I haven't been able to get any word about Patty. Was she ill? She wasn't running a temperature . . . ?"

"Running a purple snit is more like it," Mrs. Ellsworth said coolly. She had ignited her cigarette and puffed on it nervously. "Dean will tell you there isn't one thing on earth wrong with Patty that a lot of attention wouldn't cure. Or possibly she's had *too* much attention—I couldn't begin to guess. All I know is that I've had a ghastly day and an even more excruciating night trying to reason with her to stop shrieking like a banshee. I'm only human, you know. I can only take so much, and then I'm liable to go to pieces myself."

Lillian raised her hand to wave away a cloud of smoke that had been blown in her direction. "She was very disturbed, Mrs. Ellsworth. Patty's a terribly sensitive child, and she's desperately in need of . . . of attention, and. . . ." Lillian didn't use the word "love" —Carmen Ellsworth wouldn't have grasped its meaning.

"Oh, I'm *fully* aware of that, darling. Good heavens, who knows Patty if I don't know her? She's a regular little showman—anything at all to get people to notice her. And she can be absolutely adorable at times. Cute as a bug's ear. Everyone says she looks like a living doll. But, you know, there are limits. Some of us are constituted to put up with youngsters like that and some of us are simply too high-strung to be able to cope." Carmen rolled her beautifully mascaraed eyes ceilingward and released an exasperated sigh. "When I got called home from that luncheon yesterday by that ignoramus of a woman I'd hired, I tell you, my nerves were absoluely *raw!*"

She was bidding for Lillian's sympathy, absolutely certain that she was deserving of pity!

"I came home to find Patty positively uncontrollable, behaving like an absolute little savage. And this so-called practical nurse glaring at me as though I'd just set fire to an orphanage. Really! Announcing, just as though she were the Queen of Sheba, that she wasn't about to stay cooped up with a little monster who wouldn't stop screaming . . ."

Lillian shuddered, picturing the scene. "Maybe Patty was. . . ."

"Oh, nonsense. She wasn't in any pain. She simply wanted to have her way, and—I'm sorry to have to say this—but by four o'clock yesterday afternoon my nerves had just snapped. I slapped her, and. . . ."

"You *couldn't* have . . . !"

"I was sure it would calm her down." The aqua-gray eyes blinked their innocence. "Isn't that what you hospital people do when someone gets out of control? She was hysterical, and I can only take. . . ."

Lillian's rage boiled over. "Did you try cuddling her in your arms, Mrs. Ellsworth? That's what *this* 'hospital person' would have done!"

Patty's mother was unperturbed by the caustic remark. "I don't claim to be an expert on child rearing,

Miss Bryant. I certainly don't have time to make a study of it now—not while I'm going mad trying to line up a daily fashion show for one department store tearoom and another big splash for the Desert Breeze Hotel!" For a flashing instant, Carmen Ellsworth seemed to realize that in Lillian's eyes she was something less than a woman, something far less than a normal mother, and perhaps not even warm enough to be classified as a human being at all. "I'm really terribly fond of Patty," she said. "Who wouldn't be? She's precious—when she wants to be. And I've always seen to it that she was dressed. . . ."

Lillian's expression must have told Carmen that her sales pitch was not being bought; she tossed it aside hurriedly. "Oh, well, you know. It's natural to be crazy about your own child, after all." She glanced at her watch. "I hope Dean won't be too long pacifying her. He gets ridiculously disgusted when I try to tell him I have more important things to do than sit around waiting in this dreary place. I'm on Teddy Levant's interview show this morning. Have you ever caught . . . ? No, I suppose you're working when he comes on the air."

Bright chatter. Callous unconcern for whatever was going on in a room just a few yards down the corridor! *Maybe I shouldn't blame her,* Lillian thought. *Maybe something was left out of her makeup, something vital that she doesn't miss because she doesn't know it exists in other people.* She was on the verge of pitying Mrs. Ellsworth, when the latter snuffed out her cigarette and stamped to her feet.

"I've really got to run. Would you tell Dean that I'll call back later, after I get off the air?" Carmen started back toward the elevators and then turned, her magazine-cover smile as dazzling as the Arizona sunlight. She pushed the button for an elevator. "Take good care of my little doll, will you, dear? Dean and I talked it over when I brought Patty in this morning, and we're just about agreed that he should take custody. He's a little better qualified to handle a problem child than I am. *You* know—he's studied psychology and who knows *what*-all. If I had more time, I'd love to. . . ."

"I'm sure you would," Lillian said. She had turned her eyes away from the woman, giving her attention to familiar-sounding footsteps approaching from the East corridor.

An elevator had arrived and the doors yawned open. "Play along with Dean and you'll have yourself a good job for as long as you want it, Miss Bryant. He'll have to hire *someone* to take care of. . . ."

Carmen Ellsworth had stepped into the cubicle and the wheezing doors had clipped off her last bit of confidential advice. As she disappeared from view, obviously relieved to be rid of an annoying problem, Lillian could only shake her head incredulously, thinking, if ever this woman needs an operation, the surgeon's in for an awful shock. Inside, she's got to be all metal parts and plastic gears. She hadn't even waited long enough for her first husband's report from Patty's room!

CHAPTER NINETEEN

"I talked to Patty for a long time," Dean was saying. Lillian hadn't moved from her place on the waiting-room settee, but the doctor had taken Carmen Ellsworth's place. "The talking helped, and the sedation helped, but I had to make a promise before she'd go to sleep. She hadn't slept all night, you know."

It wasn't fair for him to be this close to her. Dean exuded a magnetic charge of some kind—powerful, palpable, almost impossible to fight against. "What did you promise?" Lillian asked.

"That you'd be standing beside her bed when she woke up." Dean's eyes explored Lillian's, his expression half-hopeful, half-confident. "She asked me how I could be sure. You hadn't arrived yet. I kept coming out here to check, and Patty knew you weren't around. She kept wanting to know how I could be *sure* she'd have you back when she woke up."

Like everything else that had been happening, Dean's hand reaching out to clasp her own had a dreamlike quality about it. Yet it seemed natural, too, for their fingers to intertwine, and for him to say, "I told her I knew you'd be here because I'd asked you to come back. And because you love her. That's very logical reasoning, isn't it? People who love each other don't stay apart very long. Not when one of them needs the other."

I'm going to start crying again, Lillian realized. *I'm*

going to start bawling like a ninny, and he's going to think I'm nothing but a. . . .

"Are you afraid I'm going to call on you again, and use you, and then pat you on the head like a faithful mongrel and tell you 'thanks a lot—I don't need you anymore'? Is that what you're thinking?"

She tried to think of an appropriate answer, started to form the words, and then gave up. Lillian's fingers tightened against the warmth of Dean Warner's hand.

"It's not going to happen, Lillian. Not just because Patty needs you now more than she's ever needed you. And not because that need is going to grow. Or . . . because I want to see the two of you together, for as long as . . . as long as you want to stay."

"Patty doesn't need a nurse," Lillian started to protest. "She. . . ."

"She needs a mother. She's always needed a mother. The way I need. . . ."

Lillian withdrew her hand. "Please don't. I . . . if you really want me to take care of her, I'll do it. But don't pretend that there's any more to it than. . . ."

"Than wanting a . . . an affectionate housekeeper for my little girl?" Dean's arms folded around Lillian, pulling her close to him. "That's not what I want, dearest. It took my daughter a lot less time than it's taken me to realize . . . exactly what we *do* need. Someone who loves us. Someone. . . ." Lillian's face was lifted upward so that her eyes met those of the doctor. "Someone *we* love. It's not very romantic to be talking in plurals, is it? It's just that . . . Patty found you first, for both of us. It's not easy to exclude her now."

One of the R.N.'s at the charge desk let out an audible, "Oh, *my!*" as Dean's lips closed over Lillian's. Perhaps the nurse had discreetly averted her gaze by the time Lillian's arms encircled Dean's neck, drawing him closer. It didn't make any difference. This was

126

happening! This was *real,* and it couldn't have mattered less who was watching.

A long time later, Dean lifted his head to whisper against Lillian's temple, "I thought I'd lose my mind when they told me you were gone. I didn't know until then how much I. . . ."

His embrace tightened. He was holding her as desperately as Patty had often held her. "I don't want you just to take care of Patty," Dean said. "Nurses can resign. And housekeepers have a way of quitting. Lillian?"

She pressed her face against his chest, oblivious to the clang of the elevator doors. Someone was walking past them—someone unimportant who may or may not have heard Dean Warner say, "I want you for keeps, Lillian. It's going to take some time. We'll need patience, and we'll have to do a lot more believing together. But I'm not just thinking of Patty. I'm being selfish, too. I want you for myself."

From her post at the charge desk, the head nurse made a clucking sound of disapproval.

"I *love* you," Dean Warner said. He said it clearly enough for the head nurse, and anyone else who was interested, to hear him. "I want you to marry me. I have a daughter and, legally, I've had a wife, but I've never really been married before. I've never known what it is to be *loved* before."

"You know now," Lillian whispered.

He nodded. When the morning traffic began to get too thick to allow even a semblance of privacy, Dean took her hand and pulled her to her feet. His arm circled Lillian's waist as they walked up the corridor to where a sleeping child dreamed and waited for a promise to be kept.

Other SIGNET Books by Jane Converse